*My Son, the Druggist*

*By Marvin Kaye*

BULLETS FOR MACBETH
THE GRAND OLE OPRY MURDERS
A LIVELY GAME OF DEATH
THE HANDBOOK OF MENTAL MAGIC
THE STEIN AND DAY HANDBOOK OF MAGIC
A TOY IS BORN
THE HISTRIONIC HOLMES
FIENDS AND CREATURES (ED.)
BROTHER THEODORE'S CHAMBER OF HORRORS (ED.)
BERTRAND RUSSELL'S GUIDED TOUR OF INTELLECTUAL
 RUBBISH

# *My Son, the Druggist*

MARVIN KAYE

PUBLISHED FOR THE CRIME CLUB BY
DOUBLEDAY & COMPANY, INC.
GARDEN CITY, NEW YORK
1977

All of the characters in this book are fictitious, and any resemblance to actual persons, living or dead, is purely coincidental.

Library of Congress Cataloging in Publication Data

Kaye, Marvin.
　　My son, the druggist.

　I. Title.
PZ4.K2327My [PS3561.A886]　　813'.5'4
　　　　　ISBN: 0-385-11042-1
Library of Congress Catalog Card Number 76-56309

Copyright © 1977 by Marvin Kaye
All Rights Reserved
Printed in the United States of America
*First Edition*

*To Davillah,*
*For sharing the agonies of growth*
*Yet somehow managing to laugh*

*And to Eloise,*
*For joining in the warmth of a long and hilarious*
  *friendship*
*With love*

# *ACKNOWLEDGMENTS*

Sincerest thanks to those whose invaluable aid, advice, anecdota and technical expertise made this book possible:

David M. Goldenberg, pharmacist with the Albert Einstein medical facilities in Philadelphia;

Samuel Greenberg, chief druggist and owner of Albert's Pharmacy on West Eighty-sixth Street, Manhattan, and his friend and associate,

William Siegel, president of Comu-AD Marketing Inc., public relations executive, pharmacist and contributor to pharmaceutical publications;

Dr. Nasik Elahi, senior chemist with the Office of the Chief Medical Examiner, New York City;

and the anonymous neighbor in my building who threw out an old *Physician's Desk Reference* and thus provided me with many delightful hours of cognitive skulduggery.

Those named above gave generously of their time and submitted to a doubtless wearisome barrage of questions. Any errors of fact herein, of course, are the fault of the author, who is at the mercy of notes that might stymie a cuneiformist.

Thanks also go to Eloise Goldenberg for extended hospitality, even when breakfast-table talk about the effects of toxins in the body threatened to turn her facial hue a stunning shade of green.

Lastly, special gratitude is here expressed to Julia Coopersmith for being present at the birth of Marty Gold —or at least, for his Bar Mitzvah.

*Monday, November 15*

*So, my dear Tessela,*

*This year I've finally got you! You'll bring Carol along, there's room. Every year I say, come, share a bissele bird, every year you've got an excuse. This year it's your sister's girl. Only now there's no reason not to come because my little Yossele (would you believe he's already nineteen?) won't be home on leave till late next month, so Carol can have his room, and you, you'll sleep in the new "guest bedroom."*

*"Guest bedroom!" Vey's mir, come, I need you for a buffer. Marty, my son the druggist, just moved out, which is why there's room. If you come to Thanksgiving dinner, maybe his father will keep his voice down to a shout. They're always making the mother the villain when a boy leaves home, but I've been quiet about the whole thing, while Abie— Well, you know his temper.*

*Not that I'm thrilled, either, that Marty can't stay in the same house with his parents. I'm not too ecstatic, you understand, because you can imagine the dirt and the roaches in a place he can afford. You know New York rents! And on top of everything else, he gets a roommate named Finney who's an actor yet. But do I say a word? When Marty invited us to dinner there, and before his father could explode, I* was the one who spread the oil and got them to go out to Farm Food to celebrate.

To tell you the truth, Tessela, I'm worried about Marty. I think he's questioning too much, you know what I mean. But how can I hock him in chinuck when he busted his back working through Temple? You were there, you know the story with my Abie yelling all the time, wanting him to forget everything and come into the shop with him.

Maybe Marty just moved out so he'd have room for all his records. Them, you can believe, I'm not sorry to say goodbye to!

But enough about us. I'll be glad to see Carol again, so don't you dare show up and not bring her! There'll be enough turkey to feed Coxey's army, so it is not an imposition. And tell her be sure to bring some nice things to wear.

*Love,*

*IDA*

It was bad enough that Thanksgiving was a workday and he slept through the alarm, but it was worse when he looked out the frosty windowpane and saw the streets ankle-deep in slush. And then, to top off the morning, he spied his roommate's shorts dangling demurely from the handle of the refrigerator, and that is when he began to perceive that it was not going to be the best day of his life.

*And tonight I have to eat dinner with the family and be nice to some fat shlub from Philly. She'll probably have three eyes and no tits.*

Since he didn't know whether the shorts were yesterday's or today's pair, he plucked them off gingerly, holding them between thumb and forefinger and as far away from his body as possible. Marching into the bedroom, he deposited the garment on Bill Finney's head.

His roommate snorted and turned over in his sleep.

In the kitchen, Marty Gold shaved over the sink, where the only decent mirror in the apartment was located. His mouth tasted lousy from the beer he'd been drinking the night before at the knucks session. Putting down the razor, he ran a damp toothbrush back and forth over his teeth, rinsed, then stared blearily at his own reflection. He sighed.

*Dark, oily skin. Dry hair on a big square head. Chin too big, eyes too small. Liver lips. Paul Newman you're not.*

He tried without success to comb down the cowlick sticking up in back.

Breakfast consisted of Vitamin E and Tang, mixed with lukewarm tap water. He rooted through the refrigerator, found the butter and sliced off a lump. He swallowed it so the vitamin would be able to metabolize properly.

*Reserve my compliments to the chef.*

But anything heartier would turn his stomach, for he was not a morning person. He could always pick up a doughnut on the way to work, and there was an unending supply of coffee at the pharmacy.

He debated whether he should take a hat. He hated how he looked in them, but an ad in the Sunday *Times* finally convinced him that head coverings actually served a purpose, conservation of bodily heat. Finally, he took the bushy Russian cap from the closet and shoved it in his coat pocket, hoping the weather would not warrant sticking it on his head.

*No luck.*

His breath emerged in a visible gust as he closed the street door, and his boots sank deep in sullied city snow. With a resigned shrug, he turned up his collar, affixed his cap on his skull and began to trudge off toward Eighty-sixth Street.

*At least I don't have to tuck down the earflaps.*

When he was still half a block away, he spotted the Old Lady in front of the store, her chunky figure swaying back and forth, wielding a broom like a hockey player defending home goal.

*Oh, Christ, why does it have to be today?*

But she always showed up on Thanksgiving, to help out during the holiday rush. From the end of November to the night of December 24, Etta Spector stayed in the store, sometimes round the clock. It wasn't too bad when

## My Son, the Druggist

there was a steady flow of customers, but whenever traffic grew sporadic and she had more time on her hands than the rest of the staff knew what to do with, she would think up gratuitous chores, and if she decided the floor needed cleaning, or the dump bins required dusting, it didn't matter who was handy: Art Post, the stock boy; Herbie Adelstein or Marty Gold, the pharmacists; or even her husband, Lou Spector, chief druggist. Regardless of position, the hapless victim saw it got done, and quickly.

*But Lou usually delegates the job to one of us peons.*

Marty started to enter the store, but the Old Lady blocked his path.

"I wonder, Mr. Gold," she asked, "whether you can tell me what time it is?"

The look in her eye could have liquefied lead.

"I'm sorry, Mrs. Spector," Marty apologized, head down, "I overslept. My alarm—"

"Did I say one word about that?" she snapped, drawing herself up to her full height, four foot eleven. "Did you hear me say *one single word* yet about the outrageous time you're showing up? I asked you what time it is, that's all. Is it asking too much to ask the time of day from you, maybe?"

He looked at his watch and told her the time.

"Thank you," she said with chilly dignity. "And now," she added, pointing at him with the broomhandle, "and *now*, suppose you tell me where you get off coming in so late when you should've been helping my Louie?"

"I started to tell you—"

"*Hah? I can't hear you!*" She had a convenient hearing loss, one which afflicted her mainly when she didn't want to hear what she didn't want to hear.

Just then, a loud voice from the rear of the store rescued the young pharmacist.

*"Etta, stand out of the door, damn it, and let him in!"*

Lou Spector, fat, jovial and sixtyish, with long gray hair and a ragged bristle beneath his upper lip, gave his assistant a good-natured smile and waved away the excuse for tardiness with a flip of his paw.

"Heat up some water, Marty," he suggested. "We'll be better off once Etta has her Sanka."

"You busy with the Home?"

"Yeah. They called in a rush order for this afternoon." The nearby geriatrics institution was an important, if bothersome source of income.

"Where's Herbie?" Marty asked.

"Getting a tooth yanked," Spector replied.

"On Thanksgiving? Who's open?"

"His uncle took 'im. It swelled up all of a sudden. If it don't give him a bad jaw, he'll be in around noon."

Marty groaned. "Then I have to watch the fountain all morning?"

"Who, then? *Me?*" Spector snorted.

"Yap, yap, yap," his wife yelled from the back of the store. "Get the water on already!"

Marty shed his outerwear, reached for his white lab jacket and buttoned it, hoping the Old Lady wouldn't notice the grimy cuffs. It was impossible to keep such a garment clean in Manhattan, even working indoors, but too many trips to the laundry only frayed the material.

"Louie!" she said, peering down at the floor. "When already are you gonna put new tiles?"

"Maybe you're crazy?" her husband shouted. "Who thinks of retiling in November?"

## My Son, the Druggist

"The ones in front, they're buckling."

"Sure, and they're gonna keep buckling until the customers stop slopping in slush. When it gets warm out, then talk to me about new tiles."

Before she could argue further, Spector ducked down through a raised trapdoor in the floor, stepped on the ladder-stairway to the basement and descended out of sight. The cellar was the domain of Art Post, the stock boy, when he wasn't delivering medicine, and it was also the locale of the toilet, so the pharmacist had his choice of reasons for avoiding further discussion.

Left alone, Mrs. Spector shuffled to the utility closet to put away the broom, saw Marty Gold getting the water ready for the coffee and stopped to talk at him. "Every year he says he'll retile, every year he forgets. Next spring, I'm making myself a note to remind Louie to put new tiles. I don't care what else he has to buy, they come first." She wiped her hands along the shapeless folds of her faded blue woolen skirt, and eyed the young druggist with distaste. "Marty, when you go home tonight, wash your jacket! Feh! Pigs we don't need working here!"

While the Old Lady berated Marty Gold, a few blocks away another elderly woman unenthusiastically stared out her bedroom window at the white eddies that swirled in sudden gusts against the cheerless sky.

Bernice Fenimore—one of Marty's favorite customers—regarded the new day with listless disfavor. She was in bed still, having slept little, waiting for the call, half-wishing it wouldn't come.

The phone rang and she answered it. Sure enough, it was Cohen.

"I've got positive confirmation," he told her. "Now what?"

Mrs. Fenimore sadly considered what she ought to do. Her neck was propped at an excruciating angle between headboard and bed, but she did not alter her position. She was silent so long that the voice at the other end asked if she was still there.

"I'm here, I'm here," she answered. "You'd better come over to my place tonight."

"What time?"

"I'll let you know later."

She hung up and regarded the receiver for nearly a minute before lifting it off the hook again. It took a while to get through, but when she did she was abruptly cut off because of the chance that someone might be listening in on an extension, not that she cared except maybe the story shouldn't get around by accident, so anyway she had to hang up and wait to be called back from a telephone booth.

At last she delivered her ultimatum. "So you'll be here tonight, is that understood?"

Silence from the other end.

"Maybe you don't speak plain English? I asked if you understand?"

A strangled whisper. "Yes."

"Good. Word mincing is not what I'm intending. And," Mrs. Fenimore added, "in case you have any bright ideas, I won't be alone." Who could trust a liar and a cheat, especially one backed into a corner?

Hanging up, she swung her legs out of bed and reached for her robe, shivering. To stay and fret in her cold,

## My Son, the Druggist

empty apartment was no good on such a bleak morning.

A cup of coffee, a little *schmoozing* with Marty might cheer her up. Mrs. Fenimore got dressed, put on her coat, then headed off to the drugstore for breakfast.

Spector's Drugs stands on the border of two worlds: the poor West Side of Columbus and Amsterdam avenues, and the disparate ethnic and economic mix that comprises West End Avenue and Riverside Drive.

Forty years earlier, when the store opened, the neighborhood still clung to some vestige of its turn-of-the-century glamor, but during the Second World War the most venerable households began to move away or experience the attrition of death. Landlords were forced to subdivide. The resultant smaller apartments—desirable because of disproportionately large rooms and vaulting ceilings—were snapped up by a great influx of middle-class families. Young artists and professional actors and writers, too, profoundly altered the social profile of the neighborhood . . . and incidentally, the clientele of Spector's Drugs.

The retail establishments along Broadway, from Seventy-second up as far as Ninety-sixth, also underwent sea changes. The run-of-the-mill supermarkets, *kosher* and *traife* butcher shops, dry-goods stores and stationers were jostled into providing elbowroom for art theaters, boutiques, secondhand bookshops, ethnic restaurants and craft-y cellars that would have been equally at home in Greenwich Village. Theaters grew more exotic, offering foreign films as well as family fare, silent and early sound revivals, and eventually and inevitably, a smattering of "adult" movies. The fast-food emporiums made their appearance, but were by no means restricted to Colonel

Sanders or Burger King; they included Sicilian pizza parlors, Greek gyro stands, Latinese cuchufrito counters, Israeli felafel lunchrooms, and even one reasonably authentic Texas-style *burrito cantina.*

The West Side, that of the late sixties and early seventies, was a bustling carnival of tastes and attitudes, bounded east and west by the intricate greenery of Central and Riverside parks. Marty Gold never tired of exploring the area, from the Hudson boat marina to the unexpected treasures along side streets and Broadway: the tobacco store that stocked science-fiction fanzines, the obscure second-floor 78rpm record exchange, the tiny alley of a restaurant that served only Japanese macrobiotic cuisine and Perrier water.

Spector's itself was a West Side legend, almost as famous as the miraculous Zabar's delicatessen a few blocks south. It was the last true family drugstore in the neighborhood, and still possessed its original soda fountain and lunch counter—an institution long since dismantled at other area pharmacies.

The soda fountain was both a source of pleasure and an irritation to Marty Gold. To local youngsters, he was the Brillat-Savarin of the milkshake, the Michelangelo of the ice cream sundae, and he reveled in his measure of fame, even as he regretted the temptation factor of ever-available sweets. Already he felt compelled to hold his breath and stomach in whenever passing a mirror.

*Occupational hazard of fountains: consumption on a ratio of 6:1. Make six shakes, drink one, turn into a fat pig, oink.*

But he brought considerable *brio* to his performances, aware that he was being avidly watched as he deposited the maximum credible scoop to ensure critical milkshake mass without exploding the liquid over the sides of the metal cup impossibly suspended from the Hamilton Beach blender. He constructed his confections with mathematical precision, apportioning the proper dollops of sundae topping with a twist of the wrist reminiscent of Ormandy cueing the entrance of the French horns. Because this was holiday time, the routine included a special festive halving of red and green maraschinos, disparate hemispheres pressed together, particolored ornaments to greet the season.

Because Marty held that sundae sculpting was a vanishing art, he never objected to tending fountain. But the lunch counter was another case entirely. There was no glory in slicing onions for salami sandwiches, and it irked him to have to stop in midprescription to heat up a can of chicken noodle soup.

"They made me study the wrong courses at Temple, Herbie," he occasionally complained. "If I'd only had an honest adviser, he would have made me sign up for Basic Fundamentals of Chicken Salad, or maybe Advanced Liverwurst!"

The fountain occupied the left side of the store, looking toward the rear; it ran at right angles to the far counter facing the front door. Behind that counter, prescriptions were compounded. Opposite the lunch counter and running the length of the pharmacy on the right was a series of display cases housing everything from candy and cigarettes to clocks, perfume, back scratchers, cosmetics, scales and humidifiers. Herb Adelstein kept an eye on the nondrug inventory, reordering once or twice a month and setting up promotional displays in the wide center aisle of the store. When Herb wasn't busy behind the drug counter or fountain, he might be seen unpacking complexion creams or cleansing grains, arranging wristwatches or dusting the dump bins.

His absence that morning was sorely felt by the rest of the staff. It took Marty less than five minutes to make the coffee, but neither he nor his employer finished the tepid dregs for an hour. A continuous stream of customers kept them busy till nearly 11 A.M. Spector stayed behind the prescription area, and his wife took her post by the cash register, ringing up orders, rooting through charge plates to accommodate those customers who were billed monthly. The stock boy was out of the store more than he was in it. Every time he stuck his head in through the front door, Spector would hold up a batch of bags of drugs to be delivered and the kid would grab them and walk straight back out.

Marty Gold shuttled back and forth between fountain and prescription counter, alternately preparing medicine and pouring coffee. Mrs. Einhorn bent his ear for a few minutes, asking him why he didn't call up her daughter Cynthia any more, oblivious to the fact that he'd never dated her in the first place. Later, he got some Librax for Loretta Hamilton and declined her usual suggestion to deliver it himself later. Still, he liked her enough to kibitz for a few minutes during the only lull in the morning's rush. Otherwise, he had more things to do than there was time to do them in. By ten-thirty, his feet ached and his jaw muscles were tight from stretching in his customary professional grin. He prayed Herbie's tooth wouldn't give him trouble and keep him from coming in to work.

*At least the Old Lady's so busy she's staying off my back.*

Mase O'Dwyer clumped in, sat on a fountain stool and whirled back and forth. Mase, a devotee of Marty's fountain skills, was a twelve-year-old who never knew when to shut up. His father, Juggling Joe the Jolly Jester, entertained at local parties, so naturally his son thought he, too, was a wizard.

"Marty," he yelled, "c'mere, got something to show ya." The pharmacist nodded and kept on working on the order for the Home with Spector, but the kid repeated his summons again and again until, with a sigh, Marty complied.

"Mase, I'm busy. You want something?"

"Yeah, gimme a hot fudge sundae," he said, spreading a deck of cards along the counter. "Here, pick one."

*Hot fudge sundae! With his behind he should eat Rye Krisp, period.*

Marty picked a card, looked at it, then began making the sundae, scooping up a generous dip of vanilla and releasing it into a glass dish. (Once Spector suggested saving time by replacing the glassware with metal bases that could hold disposable paper cones. Marty nearly had a fit, and the idea was dropped.)

"Bet you think this is the six of clubs, huh, Marty?" the kid asked, smugly pointing his grimy fingernail to a face-down card that lay apart from the rest of the pack.

"Yeah, Mase, that's the six of clubs," Marty said patiently, squirting the whipped-cream superstructure upon a mountain of fudge.

"Wrong! It's the card you picked!" The boy flipped it over triumphantly, revealing the king of spades.

Marty slid the sundae across the counter without mentioning he'd originally selected the three of diamonds. By experience, he knew such a foolish move would only result in seeing the whole dreary performance over again.

The front door opened. Mrs. Fenimore entered.

She was an institution at Spector's Drugs. In the old days, the proprietor himself greeted her each morning; then, later, she was Herb Adelstein's responsibility. When Marty Gold was hired, he inherited Mrs. Fenimore.

She was tall, poker-straight, a woman in her early sixties with white hair, chopped short. She dressed cheaply, and it would have required a close inspection of the rings and pins she wore to discover she was one of Spector's wealthiest customers.

She liked Marty very much. He always had time to give her an unforced smile and a word of advice, which he would offer only if solicited. He knew most of her many symptoms and problems, and she in turn occasionally prompted him to speak of his plans and aspirations. She regarded him as a private physician, confidant, confessor and surrogate son, all in one.

On his part, Marty felt sorry for Mrs. Fenimore. She was a widow with a mass of illnesses, real and imagined, and although she had four children, was quite lonely. Though he never articulated the thought to himself, he looked forward to his little talks with her each morning.

Grateful to be relieved from further service as Mase O'Dwyer's captive audience, Marty walked over to the coffee urn and drew a cup, then stuck an English muffin on the grill and waited till it was golden brown. He slid it onto a plate, brought it to her, set down the coffee and poured her a glass of pineapple juice as well.

"How do you feel this morning, Mrs. Fenimore?"

"And how *should* I feel, my Marty?" she asked, sipping her juice. "It's a terrible world I live in. Every day a new heartache, and my heart, I should tell you, can't take much more." She reached out for the muffin and winced.

"Bursitis acting up?"

She nodded sadly. "That should be the greatest of my worries. What hurts me now there's no medicine for. If there only were, what a druggist you would be."

"What's the problem?"

She shook her head. "Some things, there's no use telling."

*Gevalt! A first . . .*

She'd never refused to talk about something troubling her before. He watched her curiously as she bit into the muffin and chewed slowly, methodically.

*I could practically clock the time it takes her to eat. Bet there isn't fifteen seconds' tolerance one way or the other.*

"So what's new with your family?" he asked. "Can't they help?"

She uttered a short, sardonic laugh. "Who do you think is making me worry in the first place, Marty? My children never listen to me. And half the time I don't know if they're alive or dead, and they could care less about me. My son, Lukas, he only shows up to borrow money, and when he does, he doesn't bother to shave and you could peel off his clothes with a chisel."

She lapsed into a gloomy silence.

Marty got the Silex and refilled her cup. He knew Lukas from high school. They'd been in the same homeroom. Lukas was a gangly kid with pimples who ran around with the theater crowd. In those days, Marty was too worried about his reputation to risk making his acquaintance—

*I had enough trouble getting dates.*

—even though his sister, Melinda Fenimore, was a quiet, delicately attractive young woman whom Marty had admired mutely. But asking her for a date would have been out of the question. *She wouldn't look at me, why should she? A girl like that could date whoever she wants. And besides, Pop would've killed me.*

"Marty, Marty," Mrs. Fenimore murmured, "I should only have a young man like you in the family."

He'd heard about her children often enough, though Lukas and Melinda were the only ones he'd ever met. There were two older sisters, as he recalled, one of them married to a doctor of considerable local prominence and reputation.

Marty patted her hand and told her she made him feel practically like he *was* one of the family.

"Sure, sure, that's safe for you to say because it isn't true. But it's a lovely thing to tell me, just the same." She blotted her lips with her napkin and started to rise. Her bursitis flared and she cringed.

"Marty, maybe you could give me some Darvon? It hurts."

"Certainly," he replied. "Do you have the old bottle with the prescription number?" He knew she didn't. She never remembered the empty containers when she needed a refill. *Must have a medicine cabinet full of nearly-empty bottles.*

He climbed the track ladder, found the F file, climbed down with it and lay it on the counter. He ran his finger along the appropriate pages, seeking the original prescription number for her Darvon. He discovered it in an entry that was three years old. By rights, it should have been updated with a slip from her physician. He rapidly scanned the rest of her medical record, and found a refill entered seven months earlier, nothing more recent. It was clearly time to send her back to Dr. Paul for a new Darvon requisition, and he was just about to mention it when a new throng of customers pushed through the doors, all at once.

"Oy!" Spector murmured. "Marty, *mizhazha!*" Marty obliged by moving over, allowing more room for Spector's pill-counting tray on the cramped workspace.

*Oh, hell, let the requisition go till next time . . .*

Marty got the large Darvon container, made sure of the strength, and spilled some of the capsules on his own tray. He shoved the red-and-gray pulvules about with a wooden tongue depressor until he had the proper amount, double-checked the quantity, then prodded them into a plastic vial, capped it, returned the excess to the big container and stuck it back on the shelf. Next to him, Spector went through a practically identical set of motions.

Before he could type the instruction label, Marty had to take the store phone and reassure his mother for the tenth time that he would, yes, be at the family dinner, and yes, he would dress up for company.

Mrs. Fenimore was still waiting patiently when he hurried back to the counter, but Etta Spector was glaring balefully at him. He ignored her, reopened the pill vial and fished out one capsule. He gave it to Mrs. Fenimore along with a paper cup of water, then turned back to the most tedious part of the process, typing the label.

## My Son, the Druggist

"Marty," said Mrs. Fenimore, swallowing the medicine, "you're very good to me. Believe me, I'll remember."

"Ahh," he laughed, waving offhandedly, "it's my job."

"Naah, naah, a job in a drugstore, that's your hobby, my Marty. Your work is your jazz music, and all that."

He smiled, stopping long enough to press her hand. "That's a nice way to put it."

"And you're a nice young man. Maybe I could trade sons with your mother?"

He grabbed at the right-hand bottle of pills, stuck on the label and put it in a bag, stapling a receipt to it. "You wouldn't want me," he said, "the food bills would bankrupt you."

"Perhaps I'd be better off without so much money." She pulled a woolen scarf about her thin, wrinkled throat, buttoned her coat. "And perhaps, my Marty," Mrs. Fenimore added, a slight smile upturning the corner of her mouth, "you would be better off for a little less food, no?"

He patted his stomach ruefully. "What can I tell you? It's an occupational hazard, working in a store with a soda fountain."

"Well," she sighed, "there are worse sins than gluttony." She grasped his hand impulsively. "Marty, you're a good boy. Stay that way. Don't ever become a bum."

He almost made a joke of it, but she seemed so earnest that he dutifully patted her hand and told her what she wanted to hear.

No sooner had she departed when Herb Adelstein, the missing druggist, walked in. He took one look at the large group of customers, put his hand to his jaw and moaned in pretended pain.

"Martillah," he groaned, "suddenly my tooth grew back. I'll see you tomorrow!" He turned as if to go, but a shrill, sharp voice suddenly skewered and transfixed him.

"An hour I stand here," the Old Lady clamored, "I can't even go to the toilet while Marty plays with little Houdini and yaps like a magpie and now this shlemiel behaves like the Second Coming of Menasha! *Clowns we don't need!*"

Herb Adelstein walked meekly to the back of the store and quickly changed to his lab jacket. Marty leaned over to him and whispered, "God help you, bubbaleh, if your cuffs aren't clean . . ."

On any given day, perhaps five hundred customers might patronize a typical Manhattan pharmacy, but Spector's nearly doubled that because of the fountain-lunch counter. Traffic was even brisker during the holidays.

Thursday was the worst because the crazies came out at noon. There was a welfare clinic at Eighty-first and Columbus that treated local indigents on Thursdays; some of its patients brought their prescriptions to Spector's, where they succeeded in pushing the staff members to the limits of their tempers.

A typical example was Erasmus Tyler, a septuagenarian with grizzled hair, gaunt frame, and a pair of rimless specs perched on the bony blade that was his nose.

Lou Spector scowled at Tyler's prescription. "Damn it," he grumbled, "tell that doctor of yours to stop writing things like this. I won't fill them any more."

The old man placed his hands palm-flat on the countertop, smudging the glass. "What you mean, you won't fill? My money got warts?"

Spector gave Marty, standing next to him, a get-this-one poke and regarded the old man with a mixture of amusement and annoyance. "Look," he complained, "it takes more time to fill your order than it's worth. Who writes prescriptions for only six capsules at a time?"

"That's all the money I got," Tyler replied.

"All right, all right, so here," growled Spector, fishing into a medicine container. "Goddamned cotton! Why do they pack it in so tight? Marty, hand me the scissors." He dug the point of the scissors inside the bottle, extricated the recalcitrant cotton and shook out six pills, which he stuck into an empty container. "Here," he told Tyler, "take six and don't give me anything for them. The rest of the bottle I'm gonna send to your meshuginah doctor and if he wants to pay me, fine, if not, not—but don't come in here again with any more six-pill prescriptions!"

The old man glowered at Spector, stuck the pills in his pocket and stalked out.

"Tactical error, Lou," Herb Adelstein remarked.

"Huh?"

"You should've taken the prescription slip from 'im. Either he'll use it someplace else, or if he's dumb enough, he'll come back here when you're out. Or he might just sell it."

Prescription-peddling was an added source of harassment, one that was very difficult to guard against. Some of the poor people at the welfare clinic succumbed to the temptation of making a few dollars by selling their prescriptions for controlled substances to street hustlers—petty profiteers who built up drug inventories for marketing uptown. The three pharmacists knew the names of some of the patients prone to the practice and were wary, but more often, it was impossible to tell.

One shifty-eyed individual aroused Marty's suspicions when he held out a prescription for Tuinal that bore the name of Vanessa Waters. When challenged, however, he showed a driver's license with the same name.

"Not my fault, man," he grinned. "My momma wanted a girl."

Twenty minutes later, while Spector was in the cellar, Erasmus Tyler did just what Herb Adelstein predicted and tried to get the tall skinny druggist to fill his six-capsule prescription a second time. The argument that ensued only terminated when Spector emerged from the basement and threatened to kick his cantankerous customer in a sensitive spot.

The Old Lady had her share of headaches, too. Because she took care of the cash register, it was she who caught the initial complaints about the rising cost of medicine. "Now look," snapped one young woman, "the last time I only paid a dollar! How do you have the nerve to charge me two-fifty?"

Etta Spector shrugged. "And are you paying the same thing this month for meat that you did last summer?"

"But a dollar-and-a-half increase!"

Spector leaned over the counter and butted in. "Mrs. Halloran, listen, go to any other pharmacy anywhere in the city, you would've paid two-fifty back in August, even. A big store, they adjust prices every time the market goes up. Me, I figure it's too much trouble. I wait for old stock to run out on any drug before I bring my prices into line."

"But a dollar and a half?"

"Mrs. Halloran," he sighed patiently, "you have any *idea* how fast pharmaceuticals are going up? Codeine alone, not long ago, jumped over thirty dollars an ounce in one price hike!"

*"But a dollar and a half!"*

Gesturing helplessly, Spector gave up the conversation.

Meanwhile, Marty, still sleepy from his 2 A.M. card game, had his own problems, and his temper was not improved by exhaustion, the weather, the impending family dinner, or the presence of the Old Lady.

A testy olive-skinned woman in ratty dungarees clumped over to him. Her wool shirt had no buttons, and she wore no brassiere. The garment was inefficiently closed over mammoth breasts by a large political button, "Rush Steve Rush to Albany," which was thrust into the front edges of her shirt. Her breath was reminiscent of cooked cabbage.

"What de hell wrong that doctor?" she demanded, holding up the suppositories Marty had prepared earlier. "He no say what de hell I supposed to do with them!"

It took all his fortitude to refrain from replying.

At two o'clock, there was a slowdown in business. The Old Lady sourly announced she was leaving to shop for her husband's dinner.

*As if she doesn't eat and it's Lou's fault she has to cook.*

When the door shut behind her, the three men unintentionally sighed in unison.

"Hey, Lou," Herb Adelstein said, "what's with Etta? No holiday bird this year?"

"Aaah, I could care less. She yells she misses the kids, it's not Thanksgiving without the family, but for once I'm staying home instead of shlepping all the way to Boston, what for? to see my son-in-law, the shvuntz? Bad enough they'll all be here for New Year's!" Dismissing his clan and the holiday with a disgusted flip of the paw, Spector picked up a copy of the *Daily News*, perched on a stool in front of the fountain and read his newspaper.

Marty and Herb flopped onto adjacent chairs, worn out.

Marty Gold, five feet eight and stocky, was in marked physical contrast to his coworker, who measured one inch over six feet. But he unconsciously mitigated his height by cocking his head so far to one side that Marty wondered what it must be like to go through life seeing things sideways.

"Nu, Marty," he asked in his thin, lemon-wry voice, "what gives? Celebrating the feast?"

"I have a choice? I've got the family *schmeer* to drag through."

"Thanksgiving," Herb reflected. "Beaumont called it the one genuine American holiday because it's observed with nothing but greed and satiety."

"Huh?"

"In udder woids, Martillah, you stuffs your gut until you bust."

"Right," said Marty, poking around in his shirt pocket to locate the box of Sen-Sen he always kept there. Finding it, he shook three small squares into his hand. *The minimally accepted quantity when you reek of salami and onions.* "And this year, it's going to be worse than usual."

"How come? Because you moved out?"

"It's like this. If I walk in, my old man'd be down my throat thirty seconds after the door slams. So, to spread the oil, like she always says, my mother decides to play diplomat and invites some old yenta from Philly on the theory that guests in the house will intimidate the mad chossin, my pop."

"So what's so terrible? If you've got to do the family bit, better it should be under laboratory control."

"Na-na-na." Marty shook his head. "You don't get it yet. As long as Ida-the-mediator is going to ask a friend over, she might as well kill two birds with one invite. Tessie from Bala Cynwyd has got someone coming with her."

The other uttered a short laugh. "Don't tell me, let me

guess. Could it be someone of the female persuasion?"

Marty nodded glumly.

"Tessie has a daughter, then."

"A niece, Herbie. Name of Carol Blum."

Herb pulled an appropriately doleful face, but he spoke gloatingly. "Funny thing about names," he remarked, shaking his head. "Some are *so* appropriate. Like Blum. Listen to it. That zaftig *u* sound. The repletion of the half-barfed *Bl*. Makes it sound like *plum*, a big, fat, over-ripe purple plum. Or *plump*. Or *bum*. *Plump-plum-bum*, can you picture that? Add another syllable and you've got the start of Beethoven's Fifth. *Plump-plum—*"

"Enough already! As if my mother hasn't tried to fix me up with every cockeyed broad in Manhattan, The Bronx, Staten Island—"

"Picture this, Martillah: she'll have a forty-inch bust, but she'll only be three feet tall. You won't know whether to kiss her or use her as a footstool. Around her throat there'll be two things hanging by a chain."

"What?" Marty sighed, resigned to the ribbing.

"First a mezzuzah, because that'll make everything OK. As long as she can read right to left, that cancels out all the crap."

"All right," Marty prompted, a bit uncomfortably, "what else will she be wearing around her neck?"

"What do you think?" Herb asked. "A dog license."

Reaching down the table to take the plate of farfel stuffing from his father, Marty Gold tried valiantly to avoid staring down Carol Blum's cleavage, but failed.

His mother retrieved the platter, set it in the middle of the ample spread of food, and in the same forward movement, brought her lips close to her son's ear.

"Eyes front," she murmured, half-teasing.

Aloud, Marty said, "Boruch atoh Adonoy, elohaynu melech ho-olom, boray peree hagawfen." Silently, he thought, *Hot damn! Mom's finally come up with a winner!*

Having blessed it, Marty took a sip of the Mogen David blackberry wine and forced himself not to grimace.

*Sickeningly sweet. Good thing I laced it with vodka.*

He'd brought the pint of Nikolai on the sly as an emergency measure for staving off ennui.

But for once, the vodka wasn't necessary.

He coveted her from the corner of his eye. Carol Blum was naturally dark and sultry by design. There was a sense of half-revealed mystery about her, beginning with the deep-brown eyes and black short-cut hair curled provocatively at the temples; she heightened the effect with dark eyeshadow, long ebony lashes and a muted shade of polish on her artificial nails. She wore a low-cut black knit top involved in an identity crisis as to whether it was a blouse or a sweater, and she affected matching slacks, very snug but simple of line. She did not have any jewelry, not even a watch, but as Marty stared at her full bosom, he realized she knew she needed no excess ornamentation. As for the missing mezzuzah—

*Look, what do I want, a woman or a synagogue?*

Her features were regular and delicate, except for a pair of lips too wide to be considered beautiful. Yet as she smiled fleetingly at him, they suggested a subtly bridled sensuality that caused him to hang upon that hypothetical moment when some oblique promise might escape their scented prison.

And then, sure enough, Carol spoke to him.

"What kinda car you drive?" she asked. Her timbre and pitch, pure Oxford Circle, was the aural twin to the flat nasal twang common along the Grand Concourse in The Bronx.

Her question might have stirred a vague presentiment in the young man's subconscious, but as he posed it, Carol leaned toward him, and he noted that she was not wearing a brassiere.

"I don't have a car," he replied, grinning anxiously lest she overestimate the maximum angle she might safely bend.

"Oh," she murmured and righted herself.

"Most New Yorkers," Marty explained half-apologetically, "don't have automobiles. The garage costs alone—"

"I'm sure," Carol's aunt Tessie said sweetly, "there's no need in a city like New York that has so many subways." Was there the merest pause before she uttered the last word? as if it were vaguely distasteful to her lips?

During the long ensuing silence, Marty studied each morsel of food he ate as if prospecting for precious gems.

The tines of his fork glittered in the soft glow suffused by the cut-glass chandelier suspended over the table

## My Son, the Druggist

which his mother had spread with the damask cloth, the one with matching napkins, four of which graced the laps of the company. The fifth, which would have served little purpose on the convex paunch of Mr. Gold, was tucked tightly beneath that individual's double chin.

"Marty," rumbled Abe Gold between bites of turkey, "I hope you put out those roach traps I bought you."

"I'll get to it, Pop."

"When? On the day you wake up and find little animals playing pinochle on your nose, that's when! I didn't buy them, they should lay in the drawer!"

"Abie . . ." his wife warned, her voice low.

"It's not enough you decide to live in a dump instead of your own home," he continued, his fleshy cheeks beginning to quiver, "but you have to go and find an actor yet who doesn't even try to sweep up the crumbs and the dirt—"

"Abie! *Shah!*"

He turned to his wife, saw her lips were compressed, began to say something, thought better of it and subsided.

"Better things there are to talk about at dinner," she pronounced distinctly and slowly, waiting for the challenge that did not come. Victorious, she turned back to the kitchen to fetch another dish of food. Mrs. Gold, a diminutive woman in her fifties with iron-gray hair and a neck as thick as a chicken's, was never at rest. Scarcely would she sit down to eat when she would hop up again to refill a bowl. Her constant birdlike animation was reflected in her lips, which, when they weren't talking, twisted in a smile more nervous than mirthful.

"Ida, sit already!" her friend Tessie Besserman commanded. "Either you stop fussing and eat, or I insist on giving you a hand."

"All right, so I'll *try* to rest a minute. Pass me the peas and carrots." She took the bowl, spooned up the remainder of the vegetables onto her china plate and checked an impulse to jump up again and refill the supply.

Her son chewed his food in silence, first glancing at the now-distant young woman next to him, then at the rest of the assemblage: his father, tall, fat, with eternal five o'clock shadow on his jowls, possibly to compensate for the lack of hair on his gleaming forehead; his mother, tiny, fidgety, dressed in her fanciest housewear that was silently rebuked by the tasteless finery adorning her too-too-elegant Main Line friend. Tessie (she called herself Theresa ever since moving to Bala Cynwyd) was Ida's oldest school chum. She'd managed to stay on the trim side of matronliness over the years, but it was a battle that required constant surveillance. Though the distances of time and miles had put barriers between the women, neither would admit there was nothing much left to say to one another. Tessie condoled politely with her friend for the absence of her youngest son, Yossele, and then the women chattered of past events—long past—and debated over which old acquaintances might be grandmothers and which might be dead.

But Marty sensed the subtext beneath the stream of aimless reminiscence: the hint of victory in his mother's eyes. *At last you've visited my world!* Silently, her friend beamed back at her, *Yes—and found it wanting.*

Indeed, it was not an opulent apartment by Theresa Besserman's standards, and what was worse, the Golds' possessions failed to reflect any meaningful culture, as she

## My Son, the Druggist

knew it. Music? Rosenblatt's falsetto could *scarcely* be mentioned in the same breath as the rich countertenor of a Deller or even the thinner, yet impeccably phrased line of an Oberlin. Literature? Well, yes, there *was* Singer and Roth and Malamud and Potok and Peretz on Ida's bookshelf, but that was mere insularity. What of Capote and Vonnegut and Faulkner (oh, of course not in the same class, but one *must* be aware of the other side . . .)?

She glanced at the single painting on the wall, an unremarkable reproduction of an unremarkable rendition of a family seder, bearded patriarch in tallis lofting a glass of wine—hopefully not as god-awful as the stuff in the tumbler next to her plate.

Marty Gold ate another bite and did his best to mask the grin that tilted the corner of his mouth as he regarded his mother's friend. He wondered whether she would have been invited at all if it hadn't been for her niece, Carol.

*All right, so I'll do like Ma wants, for once . . .*

"Would you care to go out Saturday?" he asked Carol. Friday was impossible, pre-empted as it was by Sabbath services, which his father would hardly allow a houseguest to miss.

"Where 'ja want to go?" Carol asked.

Momentarily, Marty was stumped for a reply, but his mother sprang to his aid.

"After dinner," she suggested in a tone which brooked no argument, "you'll put on your galoshes and take a walk around the neighborhood, it's not too cold, and you can show Carol some of the city and decide where you might go Saturday. All right? All right." There was no discernible pause between question and answer.

So the matter was settled. At the end of the meal, Marty excused himself, went into the bathroom and tried to comb down his recalcitrant cowlick. He splashed on some of his father's aftershave, the expensive one that Abe Gold only used for weddings and funerals, and rinsed his mouth with water, checking in the mirror for food particles stuck between his teeth. The hasty toilet was topped off by the obligatory three squares of Sen-Sen.

*Would she get mad if I offered her some?*

One final half-humorous, half-displeased glance at his reflection. His eyes were his best feature—brown, expressive and direct—but he was usually too shy to use them boldly with a woman. He knew he wanted to greet Carol when he emerged from the john with a look both knowing and mature, but she had her eyes level and waiting; did he detect a faintly amused, rather superior attitude lurking behind the luster of her pupils?

They trudged in the cold air, their feet crunching the frost crystals, and tried to find things to talk about once they'd decided on plans for Saturday night. Carol had a huge assortment of anecdotes about Philadelphia friends, mostly men, and Marty politely tried to listen. But with her fur topcoat swaddling her body, there wasn't much else to occupy him as they walked, and his mind started to wander.

*Wonder if my bid'll win the Basie? Maybe I should've tacked on another penny, just in case . . .*

He stopped, suddenly embarrassed.

"I'm sorry," he said, "I guess I was in a daze."

"I asked, Where d'you work?"

## My Son, the Druggist 33

"Right over there, up Eighty-sixth near the corner of Amsterdam. Stop in tomorrow for a minute."

"Sure," she yawned, then suggested it was time to get back.

He accompanied her to the door of his parents' building and asked her to say goodnight to the others. "I've got to get up early for work."

"Sure," she said, then, unexpectedly, leaned over and kissed him on the mouth. It lasted less than a second, but it was still exciting. Before he had a chance to respond, she smiled mischievously, opened the door and slipped through.

*I'll be damned!*

The doorman was nowhere in sight, so Marty waited until she turned the corner to the elevators. He felt confused, unable to sort out his feelings about her. Giving it up, he turned and headed for home, hoping his roommate might still be awake so he could talk to him. But Bill Finney was already asleep, his snores shaking the mountain of bedclothes. The same pair of shorts were in bed with Finney where Marty had dropped them that morning, but he was too elated to notice.

*Hot damn! Wait till Saturday night!*

Two minutes after he'd left his parents' apartment house, Carol peeked around the corner of the corridor. When she saw Marty was gone, she stepped outside once more, hailed a taxi and rode off to an address one of her friends in Philadelphia had given her.

Five minutes later, a man in a dark-brown business suit left Mrs. Bernice Fenimore's apartment. There was still another person inside with her. Both were in the living room.

"No," she snapped, interrupting the other. "I've said and said, and now *genug*. You can do what you want, but if you're smart, you'll do what *I* said because I meant every word!" Her lips were pressed grimly together as she scrutinized the other with narrowed eyes.

"What's the matter, you're sick?" she asked. "You *should* be. Go!" Her arm swept in the direction of the bathroom. "You shouldn't make a mess on my rug!"

The other took her suggestion, went into Mrs. Fenimore's bathroom and closed the door.

Marty reached for his lab jacket and couldn't find it.

"Your shmotah's at the Chink's, chazzah," the Old Lady said, arms folded defiantly. "Go home, get a suit [she pronounced it "soyt"] jacket, the customers shouldn't think we're hiring hooligans."

"I should go home? What happens if it becomes busy in here? I—"

"*Hah?* I couldn't hear, maybe you said something?"

It was no good arguing with her, so he did as he was told.

When he got back, the store was jammed. He weaved in and out of a maze of elbows and knees and almost reached the prescription counter when a hand grabbed his arm.

"Marty!"

He looked down at the person grasping his sleeve, and his eyes widened in surprise.

"Ma! What are you doing here so early?"

"To you I got to talk, bum," she said, staring grimly at her son. She was wrapped in a faded wool coat with bare patches where time had been unkind to the fabric.

"It's busy today," he told his mother. "Can't it wait?"

"Nah, Marty, it can't wait."

"Something wrong?"

"He asks me is something wrong. The soul of innocence!"

Spector's gruff voice rang out. "Yo, Marty, how about it, hah?"

"Ma, look, I just can't talk now."

"A minute you couldn't give me? A *second*, even? To tell me where you would take Carol and stay out all night?"

*What's she talking about?*

"Marty, *c'mon*," Herbie urged. "We're up to our kishkas in customers!"

Mrs. Gold stood on tiptoe to catch the other druggists' attention, to tell them to wait, it was important, but it was a physical impossibility for her to stretch so far.

Just then, the phone rang. Herb picked it up, called out to Marty that the call was for him. Grateful to have an immediate summons, he pulled away from his mother, rounded the counter and accepted the phone.

"Hello? What? You'll have to speak up, I can't hear you."

"It's Carol," the voice at the other end whispered. "Marty, do me a favor, okay? If anybody asks, we were out all night, okay? I'll explain later. G'bye."

The line went dead.

*What in holy hell is going on?*

"Look, Marty, busy or not, I don't care, I want to say two words to you!" His mother squeezed between a fat man and Mase O'Dwyer and entered the work area of the store. Spector glanced up, ready to bark at the intruder, but when he saw who it was, he smiled overaffably.

"Mrs. Gold, hello, how nice! You know my wife, Etta?"

"Thank you," said Mrs. Gold with politely precise enunciation, "we have met before, yes."

Etta Spector nodded to her, asked about her younger son and when he would be home from the army, and she and Spector listened with interest while Mrs. Gold replied and six customers waited impatiently for the business of the store to start up again.

"So how's Marty working out?" his mother asked, as if he weren't in the room, and in spite of the fact that she was piqued at her son. "His father and I are very proud of him."

"More young men there should be like him," said Mrs. Spector, regarding him with a peculiar look. "A good, clean boy."

Marty stared at her, astonished.

The amenities over, the proud woman dragged her son off to the far end of the cosmetics display, then poked a bony finger in his ribs for emphasis.

"I would like to know," she declared, "what kind of gentleman is it keeps a guest in his parents' home out till 5 A.M. the very first night he meets her?"

"*What?*"

"Mr. Innocent on me don't play! Is this a way to behave, Marty? I'm so embarrassed Tessie should say something, I'm afraid to look her in the eye! The first night, Thanksgiving, you had to cause a scene?"

*I'm in a pecan factory!*

"Ma, *what* scene? I didn't—"

"Nah, of course not when you were there, you didn't cause it, but after, when Carol called to say you were staying out, you should've heard your father. *You* should've, not me! Thank God, he went to bed, never found out how late you brought Carol back! Marty, I ask you, why would you embarrass me like this? You couldn't wait till Saturday night?"

He had his protest framed, but his mother's phrase brought him up short.

Saturday night. Don't mess it up, bubbaleh.

"Uh, Ma," Marty said slowly, "look . . . what can I say? I'm sorry."

"Sorry I don't need. Sorry is too late."

"Did Carol say anything?"

"What should she say? She's in bed, exhausted, and your father wanted to know why she wasn't at breakfast, but never mind. As far as I'm concerned, nothing happened, and you'll do me the favor of not alluding to last night, because your father doesn't need new reasons to holler his head off at you. *Genug.* And *shecket. F'shtay?* Tonight you'll meet us at the house for services. Be on time."

He pretended it was a question. "All right, I'll meet you."

"And wear a tie. No fancy dickeys, please, your father shouldn't have a heart attack during the boruchas."

"*Marty!*" Spector's regard for Mrs. Gold's presence had dissipated. "*Get your ass over here already, will ya?*"

"What's wrong with you?" she berated her son. "The man pays you, he shouldn't have to holler for you to work. Go, shlep!"

"For Chrissake," Marty exploded, "is it my fault I'm not—"

"You're going to waste *more* time arguing?"

"*Marty!*"

He took a breath, stifled his comments, and walked behind the counter. He didn't see his mother leave.

The store stayed busy for another thirty minutes, then there was a lull. Marty refilled Loretta Hamilton's Chlor-Trimeton, took her money and bid her goodbye. The

## My Son, the Druggist

blonde smiled, and stared at Marty longer than was necessary. As she departed, Herb nudged his friend.

"Good stuff, Marty, whyn't ya ask her out?"

*Forty times a week he asks me.*

"Look, Herbie, if you've got the hots for her, *you* ask her."

"Kid, it's you she wants. One of these times she'll jump across the counter and grab you by the mortar-and-pestle."

"Sure, sure."

"What's the matter with her? Because she's a shicksah?"

"Herbie, drop it, okay? I want to ask whether you and Betty might want to go double tomorrow someplace."

"Sure. Who you taking?"

"Carol."

"*The* Carol? Of Blum-bum fame?" Herb spoke from the side of his mouth, an affectation of his when he wanted to sound clever. He'd picked it up from watching Damon Runyon characters in old movies.

"You'll be surprised when you see her," Marty observed.

"So she's not from Dogpatch?"

Marty took a taste of coffee, made a face, poured it down the sink and replaced it with a fresh cup. As he did, he described Carol Blum in lingering detail.

"So where were you thinking of going tomorrow, Marty?"

"Thought I'd leave it up to her. Visitor to New York, you know . . ."

"Uh-huh."

"Listen, Herbie . . . there's something else."

"About Carol?"

"Yeah. It's been bugging me all morning."

"So? Shoot."

Reluctantly, Marty described the incident of the phone call and his mother's visit. "What do you think?" he asked. "Should I have covered for her?"

Herb shrugged. "Depends. Personally, I'd dump her."

"Yeah, that's easy for you to say, but—"

"But she's hypnotized you with her body. Nu, so take her out, Martillah, see what you can get, and I'll bet it's a handshake. Better *not* leave the choice of where we're gonna go up to her, though. She'll pick someplace that'll cost us an arm and a leg."

"You can't know that."

"Marty, Marty, I know this kind of broad. The Main Line princess. For starters, she's used to expensive dates. For another thing, if she can't go out with Robert Redford, she'll make sure the poor shlub that *does* escort her pays for the privilege. She sounds like one real dog!"

"I *told* you she looks like a young Elizabeth Taylor!"

"Man, there are dogs and dogs. This one's a psychological canine, a real yenta cocker bitch."

"You know what, Herbie?" Marty asked. "I think you're prejudiced."

"*Me?*"

"It's a thing with you, if a girl doesn't have a *Mc* or *Mac* in front of her last name—"

"Hey! *I'm* prejudiced? *You're* the one who never goes out unless your date has a nose like a garden hose."

"See? That kind of wisecrack is what I'm talking about!"

"Marty, look, I don't give a good damn what a person is, one way or the other. Only it's harder in our crowd to find women who don't have fifty million hangups. You ought to know that, you, of all people. Why did you move out in the first place if it wasn't to get the whole ethnic albatross off your neck—"

"That's not the way it is at all!"

*Isn't it?*

The phone rang. Spector picked it up, said a few words, then gestured for Marty to take it.

"Fenimore," he said.

"Hello, Marty," the old woman whined. "I don't feel too great. Like when I got a reaction once. All itchy, and it's hard to breathe."

"Anything else, Mrs. Fenimore?"

"Yeah, my stomach feels not too terrific."

"I'll call Dr. Paul, he's just up the street from you."

"I already phoned, he's on an emergency, who knows when he can come? Maybe you could stop over, instead?"

"I'll try, but we're liable to get busy any minute, you know how it is during the holidays."

"I understand. Come when you can."

He hung up, got the ladder, mounted it and looked for her file. Below, Herb continued to talk.

"That *is* why you never asked out the Hamilton dame, isn't it, Martillah? Because she's a shicksah."

"Herbie, I've got enough troubles with my old man without extra aggravation. And for your information, I moved out so I could have a place to take girls, that's number one, and number two, so I could have a place to put my records." He lugged the appropriate box down the ladder and put it on the edge of the long prescription-compounding counter.

"Sure, sure, Marty, whatever you say."

*Shut up, Herbie.*

He scanned the close-set typed lines in the medical history resumé of Mrs. Fenimore. The only allergic substance noted was phenylbutazone, but it was almost a year earlier that she'd had a prescription filled for Butazolidin Alka . . .

"Something wrong with Fenimore?" Spector rumbled, picking a tooth with his thumbnail.

"She ever have an allergic reaction?"

Spector nodded. "About a year ago. Sterazolidin or one of those phenylbutazone medicines."

"Butazolidin, according to the books."

"Yeah?"

"She says she's feeling like she did then. Itchy, nervous stomach, shortness of breath."

"Yeah, but naah—she don't take Butazolidin, not any more, not after *that* reaction. Doc Paul, that quack, said it was the most violent he'd ever seen, considering it was a first dose. The shvuntz never shoulda prescribed that stuff for her, not with *her* history of complaints."

"Yeah, but what do you think—"

"What's she on for her bursitis now?" Spector anticipated Marty. "Darvon?"

"Yep."

"Okay, that's what it must be. That stuff can give you a skin rash once in a while, sometimes an upset stomach, nothing serious. Give 'er a call, tell her to lay off the Darvon till she can get a prescription for something else."

Marty did as Spector suggested, but there was no answer.

"Maybe she's on the way over," Spector said. "If it

doesn't get too crowded all of a sudden, maybe you should go peek your head over there, hold her hand, if she doesn't show up in ten or fifteen minutes."

But it did get too crowded.

He remembered his promise on the way home from work. Though she lived in the opposite direction, he detoured toward her house.

A bitter wind off the Hudson chapped his cheeks and made his lips tingle as he rounded Eighty-sixth and walked south on Riverside Drive. He stopped at a plush apartment building and saw Cholly Gallagher, proud in his epauletted jacket and braided cap, standing in the middle of the sterile decorator lobby that no one ever sat in.

*The dope found his level.*

He got the job of doorman shortly after graduating the same class as Marty Gold. They had not been close in high school; in fact, Gallagher had been a constant source of harassment. But the world had intervened, economic lines were drawn between the two, and Cholly evinced a grudging civility toward his former schoolmate.

Cholly (actually Charley, but he pronounced it with a Jersey accent) was a sloppy young man of medium height with a roll of baby fat at his waist that needed a few more seasons to qualify as a beer belly. His curly, uncombed hair and bland, ruddy coloring contributed to the impression that his was the untidiness of unformed adolescence, that time would add character and dignity to his features. It was an illusion, one that would fade when the gray that dallied with his brown hair declared itself in earnest.

*As much character as a slab of lard.*

Marty couldn't stand him.

"Yo, Mart," he said, sawing the air with one hand in salutation. "How they hangin'?"

"Is Mrs. Fenimore out?" Marty saw no reason to say any more than was necessary to his old enemy.

"Old bat ain't budged all day, far's I know. I'll ring." Gallagher punched a call button, then winked at the other. "Hear she's rich, Mart."

"So what?"

"So," he shrugged, "I shouldn't hafta tell *you* about money, how to get it, huh?"

*One of these days I'm going to break his nose. I only wish.*

(Abe Gold, despite his religious role in the community, was a boxing fanatic, but Marty's mother never permitted him to learn "how to take care of himself." Once Pete Meyers had him put on boxing gloves, and Marty got thoroughly clobbered. Of the incident, Ida Gold said, "Good. A nice Yiddish boytchick uses his mind, not his paws, like an animal. That's for the shkutzim!" She never explained the advantage of standing there and being beat up on, though. Marty always felt he must have missed part of her lecture, the most important part.)

Cholly Gallagher released the call button. "She don't answer. Gaw head up."

He unlatched the lobby door. Marty stepped through, summoned the elevator and rode to the twelfth floor.

A long corridor ran both ways from the point where he got out. The Fenimore apartment was to the left and at the far end, a gray door that was the termination of the gray hallway in that direction. Marty started toward it.

A door just in front of him to the right opened and a young woman stepped into the hall carrying a bag of trash. She had on a blue quilted bathrobe and furry slippers, and her blond hair fell below her shoulders. She was beautiful.

It was Loretta Hamilton.

"Why, hello, Marty!" she said, pleasantly surprised. "You come to see me?"

"I . . . I didn't even know this . . . this is where you live," he stammered. He tried to edge past her, but there was no way to do so without brushing against her ample bosom.

"Would you do me a favor and hold the incinerator door for me? It's awful heavy."

"Sure," he replied, fidgeting nervously. He followed her as she walked down the corridor, buttocks swaying provocatively, deliberately. She indicated a heavy metal portal; he grasped the knob, turned it, held it open. The blonde reached within to tilt open a bin door, and as she did, the front of her robe fell open. Disposing of the trash, she clutched the material of her robe demurely shut and stared at Marty with a frank smile.

"Afraid I've been a little immodest, by accident," she laughed, dimples deepening in her cheeks.

It confused him. Was she really embarrassed, or was she flirting? Maybe she was mocking him? *All of the above? None of the above?*

"Stop in a minute and have a drink, why don't you?" she asked.

He tried to say no, but her eyes held his and the word stuck. His father flashed into his mind, was replaced by Carol Blum's image . . .

*A psychological dog, Martillah!*

"Come on, Marty," she coaxed, putting a hand briefly on his arm. "One drink won't take long."

The age-old threnody of guilt was hammered down by an equally venerable emotion. *What the hell?* he thought, *What the hell?*

When he re-emerged from Loretta Hamilton's apartment, there was only one thought in his mind.

*Christ, I'll never make it on time!*

To get to his apartment and change—never mind about dinner—and meet his parents for Friday night services was barely possible. He trotted down the hall, stabbed at the bell of Mrs. Fenimore's apartment, waited, rang a second time, got no reply, gave up and raced back toward the elevator.

Cholly Gallagher was in the back hall, sweeping, so he didn't see Marty Gold get out of the car and enter the lobby.

*Pushing a broom. That's the dope's speed.*

Glad to avoid a second confrontation, Marty softly and quickly crossed the lobby and let himself out the front door.

He tried to run all the way home, but got winded after half a block and had to rest. From there on, he confined himself to a brisk, aching walk.

Bill Finney was awake for a change, rummaging through the refrigerator. When he heard his roommate enter, he clicked his heels together, grinned broadly and made a deep bow from his waist, hands together, palm to palm.

"Most esteemed Herr Gold," he said as if invoking him, "I bid thee welcome."

"How much, Bill?" Marty groaned.

"Just enough," the other grinned even more broadly, "to get a pack of papers. I'll roll the gunpowder tea, and smoke it. Decidedly euphoric, Mein Herr!"

Marty laughed, tossing him a five-dollar bill. "Why I should support your habit, God only knows, the exhaled smoke is going to give me emphysema! Here, treat yourself to a couple of tins of Balkans."

Marty had stopped smoking two years earlier and still missed the taste of the more exotic cigarettes he affected to like. Helmars, from Egypt, which his father raised the roof over. Phantoms, the first king-size-plus, before the extra length grew popular. Incredibly expensive Balkan Sobranies, smoothest and most extravagant of smokes . . .

"Your mother phoned," Bill Finney said. "She warns you not to be late. Quote unquote." He turned back to the refrigerator and withdrew a bottle of Coke, uncapped it, and swallowed it in one long pull.

*I swear his Adam's apple never moves!*

Bill Finney, standing fully upright, measured over six feet toward the ceiling and nearly half that horizontally. A straggly excuse for a mustache dipped at the corners like some 1940s oriental film villain. When he bothered to put clothes on at all, they never quite held together. His shirts hung loose, his socks turned down from a lack of working elastic at the tops. His pants were khakis or Levi's, rarely anything else, and he did not own a belt.

*But he's got a good heart.*

"What's up, Marty? Friday night services?"

"Uh-huh," Marty grunted, hopping into his suit pants.

"Don't you ever get tired of them?"

"Sure. So? You ever get tired of Mass?"

The other snorted. "I haven't been to church in years.

## My Son, the Druggist

If I'm lucky, I'll stay out of them altogether unless I drop dead while I've still got relatives to mumble over me."

Marty knotted a tie, pulled on his jacket. "Mr. Atheist, huh?"

"Atheist? That's just an imprecise label. Says the atheist in that Menasha Skulnik play I worked lights for once: 'I don't believe in God,' and then he looks heavenward and adds, 'So how you like that, huh?'"

"Then what are you? Agnostic?"

Finney scoffed. "Another label! 'Sir, are you an agnostic?' 'Well, to tell you the truth, I am not sure . . .'"

A slight, perplexed frown crossed Marty's face and was instantly gone. He wrapped his scarf around his throat. Glancing into the mirror, he had one more bout with the cowlick.

"So what the hell *do* you call yourself, Bill?"

The other executed his quasi-oriental bow. "An actor, Mein Herr Gold. An actor . . ."

On the way to meet his family for services, Marty had a mental dialogue with the absent Herb Adelstein. The subject, of course, was women.

*So is that all there is? I like your looks, so . . .*

In various guises, he'd asked it before of the real Herbie. The answer was always the same:

"Don't knock it if you ain't tried it, Martillah."

*But I've tried it. So what? Loretta's attractive, but she's no answer.*

Marty's mental Herbie: "Answer to what? I didn't hear the question!"

*Things.*

"Care to be more specific?"

*Hell, I don't know. I mean, what do you expect, here I am almost thirty, shouldn't I be thinking about a mature, a meaningful relationship?*

"Define your terms, bubbie. Is it maturity or meaning you'd be wanting?"

*Either. Both. Isn't sex supposed to be better when you're in love?*

"Then what you're really after is romance. Palpitations. Rachmaninoff. Rings through the nose."

*No, no, I'm not ready to take on someone else's life, mine is still too sloppy around the edges. But why can't I at least spend my time with a girl with brains and a nice personality?*

"A properly brought-up Jewish virgin princess who only has thighs for you."

*Is that what I'm looking for?*

"That's what you're conditioned to look for. The fact that you're not married yet according to your parents' expectations—"

"Two more minutes," snapped Mrs. Gold, "and I'd've given you up for lost!"

Marty jerked his eyes up from the carpet he'd been treading, the one running along the corridor where his parents' apartment was situated. His mother stood in the portal, a reproachful look on her thin face.

"Your father went on ahead, which is just what I didn't want. I wanted you to be here on time so we could all go to shul together, like a family."

Marty began to apologize, but she gestured impatiently and told him to "shah." Then she called through the doorway. "Tessela! Carol! Come!"

Theresa Besserman was elegantly overdressed for the unpretentious temple where Abe Gold served as part-time cantor. Carol was more conservatively attired in pale-green jacket and skirt, white sweater with high collar, matching gloves and shoes.

She smiled tentatively at Marty, and spoke in a tone only he could hear. "Okay if we sit together?" she asked. "You can nudge me when I start to doze."

*A psychological dog, Martillah . . .*

He wasn't sure whether she was alluding to the lack of sleep she must have had, or the potential dullness of the prayer session, but he agreed, somewhat stiffly. He refused to give her the satisfaction of asking where she'd been all night.

Later, in the synagogue, after he sat down from silently

reciting the Amidah, he noticed her chin starting to droop on her breast.

*The dumb broad is actually sleeping!*

He toyed for a second with the idea of letting her snooze all the way off the hard wooden bench, but just then he saw his father's fierce stare sweeping over the congregation, and mercifully, he woke her.

Beth Jeshuron, like the surrounding neighborhood, had succumbed to the erosion of time and changing clientele, and the fact that Carol sat next to him on Friday was vivid proof. Begun as an orthodox synagogue (and still one in name to appease the oldest members), it had subtly altered its philosophy to a more conservative posture. Rabbi Nathaniel Chomsky, a former theatrical agent, felt it more important to bring the congregants together in a combined liturgic-social format than to let the building remain three fourths empty for all but High Holy Days. So he introduced more and more English into the services and (not withstanding bitter arguments from Abe Gold) began to "program," as he put it, new hymns with chorale-like melodies more familiar to the Western ear than the traditional Eastern melismatics. "More fermatas," he would tell his cantor. "The congregation'll sing together better, and it'll boost the house!" Abe Gold refused to give in on the point. In other ways, though, the rabbi was decidedly successful in his modification plan. The most radical change he instituted was to permit women to sit on the main floor with the men instead of in the balcony that ran around three sides of the building like a congressional gallery. The seating question was a bitter one, and had nearly been responsible for cancellation of the rabbi's contract, but the final ballot went in his favor by a margin of eight votes, all of them said to be influenced by women. Afterwards, a *de facto* split was inevitable, but Chomsky had it all planned. Friday night services were lengthened and stressed, untraditionally (except in suburban America), as the principal weekly worship session. Middle-aged members and their children, those who practiced little in the way of household ritual, enthusiastically responded to the de-emphasizing of the "inconvenient" early Saturday morning service.

So Saturdays, the temple was sparsely occupied; the dwindling number of old, original synagogue members barely made up a *minyan*—the requisite ten men that custom demanded be present before the ritual could begin.

Marty Gold took a seat in the first row. He felt as if he'd just risen from the uncomfortable bench. There were less than twelve hours between the end of the Friday evening service and the start of the Saturday morning one.

*I might as well've slept here overnight.*

Spector's Drugs was closed on Saturdays, but Marty had been pressured the night before to join his father in the morning, even though he would rather have slept.

Abe Gold mounted the three steps leading to the altar and began to don his prayer shawl. Marty removed his own tallis from the box, mumbled the line of Hebrew blessing written on its golden border in raised letters, and wrapped it about his shoulders.

The rabbi was late, but Sam Farber took over. Farber was a frail little man in his eighties. His finger shook as it skimmed along the prayer book open on the lectern before him. His thin voice also quavered.

*Why he needs the book I don't know. He knows it by heart.*

Marty was glad Farber was leading the group in prayer. If it were the rabbi, chances are he'd slow things down with English responsive reading and interpretive commentary. But any of the old men like Farber stuck strictly to the Hebrew, reeling it off in singsong monotony, faster than the most adept speed reader could possibly follow.

*Farber's the fastest, I'll be out by eleven, thank God.*

The rabbi arrived in time to draw the strings on the ark and remove the Torah. He spoke for a few seconds to the cantor, and Farber then glanced over the group, fixed his eye on Marty and gestured to him with a crook of the finger.

Marty groaned inwardly. *Christ, why me?*

Gold was not a likely name for a *kohain*, a descendant of the ancient Israeli high priests. Marty's grandfather, Yitzchak Godolkin, derived his family name from a contraction of the Hebrew words for "high priest," but when he came through Immigration at Ellis Island a bored official Americanized and constructed it to Isaac Goldol, sticking in an extra "l" by accident. Later, Isaac decided to shorten it to Gold.

Marty stepped forward, kicking off his shoes before walking on the carpeted platform of the altar, wondering for the fiftieth time what the real meaning of the shoeless business was. At odd times, he'd been told that (1) shoes were dirty (his mother); (2) stepping on the altar with the mud of the streets was disrespectful (his Sunday-school teacher); or (3) in ancient times, the power of the Almighty flowed through holy things and to tread upon the altar without shoes gave one the opportunity to soak up heavenly puissance (a Gentile professor of Bible literature lecturing at PCP's Hillel). The latter rationale seemed most plausible, since it explained the Old Testament tale of the unfortunate who brushed against the ark and died of too much God-juice (as Herb Adelstein put it) and also provided a reason for the use of the yamulka: a skullcap to prevent Divine Spirit from leaking out the fontanelle.

*But then, how come we don't take off our socks, too? Maybe they're semipermeable and allow osmosis? The whole thing's weird. But so's transubstantiation.*

"Hello, Martin," the rabbi said. He never called him Marty. He shook his hand in a grip as flaccid as a week-old flounder. "You seem to be the only *kohain* here this morning, so you'll have to take the first Torah portion."

Marty nodded and went to the side of the podium, waiting for the moment when he would be expected to recite a section of the Hebrew biblical law. He always felt hypocritical, or at least unworthy to do so.

The most embarrassing moment was always afterwards when he stepped down from the altar and put his shoes back on. Two or three of the eldest, most devout men in the first row invariably made it a point to step forward and shake his hand.

*I wouldn't mind if they were just congratulating me for managing to remember all the Hebrew. But they always look so reverent, like they want to kiss my signet ring, me, the shicksah-shtupper . . .*

The services finally came to an end, and, after begging off from a lunch invitation from his father, Marty hurried back to his apartment. He still had the afternoon to work at the library.

What Mrs. Fenimore had said was true. He regarded

his true occupation the mining of rare Dixieland and jazz music for the discerning collector. He'd entered pharmacy because of the security it provided; his early memories were rife with cold nights and little to eat. But now that the novelty of gainful employment had worn off, his thoughts turned more and more to the old music and personality recordings he'd gathered over the years from junk shops and secondhand stores. When Dick Napoleon suggested they go into partnership releasing private-label jazz discs, Marty jumped at the chance. Their first release was a moderate success, and the second album, not yet completed, already had a sizable mail-order advance sale. It was Marty's job to research the individual selections and write the jacket-liner notes. The task was not easy. It meant hours spent in out-of-the-way archives and collections. The latest task was to find cinematic information on an obscure Elmer Snowden musical short entitled *Smash Your Baggage.*

He stopped in his apartment long enough to pick up the Elmer Snowden file. As he opened the door, the phone was ringing, but by the time he reached it, all he heard was the dial tone. He checked the mail to see whether there was any news on the half-dozen record auctions he'd entered bids for, but found nothing but bills and appeals from charities.

Marty tucked the Snowden folder under his arm and left. A minute after he was gone, the telephone rang again.

When Marty returned late in the day he found a note from Bill Finney:
CALL YOUR BOSS!
*On a Saturday?*
Spector didn't answer his home phone. Marty smiled, remembering his employer's custom of taking his wife for a "little walk" every Saturday, sometimes as far as 106th, occasionally down to 72nd. "We'll work up an appetite, and go eat wherever looks good." They'd been doing it for years, and still found new restaurants from time to time.

*Funny. They close the store religiously, pun intended, but they'll eat Saturdays practically anywhere, kosher or not. I have to ask Lou about that sometime.*

Marty's taste in food was not rigorously bound by dietary custom. He would eat and enjoy a shrimp cocktail or a ham-and-cheese sandwich without a second thought. And yet a pork roast would have turned his stomach, if he had thought about it, which he didn't. He never considered the contradiction.

Cars were another thing entirely. If he didn't want his father to have a fit, he would have to wait till Saturday sundown before picking up Carol. Herbie was driving, and wheels were *verboten* on the Sabbath.

*Crazy.* Maybe in the old days it was a real labor to saddle up a pack animal, but a car was neither animated flesh nor a chore to put into motion. That's what Herbie told him once, when he was going through his reform phase of Judaism, before dropping out entirely . . .

The downstairs doorbell rang. Marty walked over to the wall button, pushed it for a few seconds and hurried to throw on a suit. It only took a minute to manage it, but he had to toss his clothes around in the manner of his roommate.

*The hell with it. He's not sarcastic. He'll never mention it.*

The knock on the door came a scant instant after the phone began ringing.

"Yo, Herbie, wait a second," he yelled, and picked up the instrument.

"Marty, that you?" It was Spector. "I been trying to get hold of you all day!"

"Yeah, hang on, I'll be right back, Herbie's outside."

The voice on the other end squawked in protest, but Marty, ignoring it, went to the front door and admitted his friend and co-worker.

"Y'almost ready?" Herb Adelstein asked. "Betty's in the car, driving around. We couldn't get a space."

"Yeah, I'm ready, but Spector's on the phone."

"On Saturday? What the hell's he want?"

Marty shrugged, then picked up the phone a second time.

Spector's voice sounded urgent. "Marty, meet me at the store."

"I tried calling you at home, Lou, but—"

"Yeah, I couldn't stand it any longer since they came this morning. I had to check things over again."

"What're you talking about, Lou? Who came this morning?"

"I don't want to discuss it over the phone. Come over to the store and hurry up."

## My Son, the Druggist

"Look, Lou, I've got a date waiting—"

"So she'll wait ten more minutes. *Come!*"

Spector hung up. Marty stared at the phone, perplexed. "What's up, Martillah?"

He made an I-don't-know gesture with his hands. "Lou sounds like his truss shrank. We've got to go over to the pharmacy."

"The pharmacy?"

"He's waiting for me there."

"Christ, we'll miss the opening credits! I hate that!"

Marty made a roaring sound and repeated it twice, turning his head as he did.

"What the hell's *that* supposed to be?" Herb asked.

"The M-G-M lion. Satisfied? Now let's get over there!"

"She's dead."

"*What?*"

"Plotzed. Aufgespielt. Dead."

"Just like that?"

"Just like that, Marty."

"How?"

"Anaphylaxis. Plus she had high blood pressure, and her heart couldn't take the edema."

"*Allergic reaction?*"

Spector nodded.

"But how? Not the Butazolidin! She knew she was allergic!"

"That's what I told 'im."

"Who?"

"The cop."

Marty exhaled, puffing out his cheeks like the personification of Wind on old sea charts. Spector sat on a fountain stool, tugging worriedly at the bristles of his iron-gray mustache.

"Could it've been anything else? The Darvon?"

"Naah. Who knows?"

"If it was Butazolidin, how'd it get in her?"

Spector shrugged. "Maybe she took it deliberately."

"Aaah, come on, Lou, you know better. She had a 365-day-a-year depression, no better, no worse. Or even if it was worse, she *had* an allergic reaction like you told me, and nobody who's been through a severe one's going to deliberately choose that way to go, you can't tell me."

"'Even if it *was* worse?'" Spector asked, cocking an eyebrow. "Figure of speech? Or do you know something?"

Marty ran his finger back and forth along a crack of the marble fountaintop. "I guess she did seem more glum than usual, last time I saw her. But why, I don't know."

The two stared into space.

"Wonder drugs," Spector murmured at length. "All started maybe twenty-five, thirty years ago, I was invited out with a bunch of druggists. Behind a Schenley plant in Syracuse, muddy field we hadda trek through to see this stuff they got outta bread mold. Buck a bottle they were asking. The stuff stank."

They were silent for a time.

"Marty."

"Mm?"

"The old pills, the original prescription that gave her the reaction last year."

"Yeah?"

"She still had all of it."

"Christ! How do you know?"

"Cop said so. But I'm supposed to go over tomorrow morning and verify the stuff in her medicine chest that we prepared. Double-check the labels, see if the proper precautionary stickers were attached, and so on. You'll go with me and help."

"Sure," said Marty unenthusiastically.

"Why the hell'd she want to hold onto that bottle of Butazolidin Alka? First time she had a reaction, Doc Paul, that klutz, hadda hospitalize her. After she got home, she was still rubbing salve and taking sitz baths for weeks.

The works. Me, I'd've flushed the damn pills down the john!"

"She never threw out medicine."

"Huh?" Spector asked. "How do *you* know?"

"Just an educated guess. You used to hand-hold her, Lou. Wouldn't you figure the same?"

"Pill hoarder? Yeah. I guess."

"Who found the body?"

"Her son, Lukas, came by to borrow some money."

"God!"

"Some surprise, huh?" Spector swiveled round on his stool. "Look, you've got to go. Tomorrow morning, meet me in front of her building, first thing."

"Right." Marty checked his watch. "Yeah, I've got to run. My date's waiting."

"Go, Marty, have a good time."

Marty gave his boss an odd look. *Is he being sarcastic?*

"So long, Lou."

*But why should he be?*

"G'night, Marty."

"Why so glum, scum?" Herb asked as Marty got back into the car.

"Nothing."

"He calls you out special on a Saturday and you say it's nothing?"

"I don't want to talk about it."

"Suit yourself," Herb grunted, putting the idling car into drive gear and pulling out into traffic.

They were all dressed casually, Marty in a brown sports jacket and darker brown pants, and a green mock-turtleneck dickey beneath a plain white shirt. Herb's windbreaker hid a similar outfit in gray and with an open collar. His semi-fiancée ("It's not an engagement, Marty, it's an understanding") wore a stylish ensemble of neckerchief, blouse and slacks; her coffee coat contrasted pleasantly with her matching bag and shoes. Betty Renninger did not believe in sacrificing appearance to comfort, so her clothes, paid for by an indulgent father, combined both qualities, but subtly and tastefully.

As for Carol Blum . . .

"My God," Betty murmured, looking out the window at Marty escorting Carol to the car, "where does she think we're going?"

The weather was mild and Carol had the front of her coat unbuttoned. As she walked, it billowed out and back, revealing an orange-and-black sateen pants suit half a size too small for her. Each leg was slit high, showing a quantity of flesh; the bodice did the same.

"She must be freezing her tail off," Herbie observed.

Carol was all enthusiasm as she climbed in the back seat before Marty. "Herbie, I'm very pleased to meet you, Marty told me everything about you and you're Betty, of course, God, I'm so damn glad to get out of that house! I feel like I'm on parole!"

"Uh . . . did my father see—" Marty began, but couldn't find the words to finish.

Carol laughed. "Hell, no, I've been Little Miss Demure for your family, but thank God, Tessie is no Gestapo, otherwise I wouldn't have gotten out without a big tsimmis. I just put on my coat in the bedroom—she brought it to me —and I buttoned up tight and left." She exhaled with a sense of relief. "Got a cigarette, Herbie?"

"Sorry, we'll all unhooked."

"*All* of you?" she asked as if they were joking. "Well, if you don't want me to start chewing the seat covers, you'd better stop where I can buy some!"

She laughed.

*Too loud.*

Herb and Marty both winced.

Marty wondered what Loretta Hamilton was doing.

Carol got out and ran to a grocery for cigarettes. The others sat and waited. Herb fiddled with the radio dial, tuning out a commercial for Steve Rush, the local attorney trying to snatch the incumbent's seat as Committeeman. "You mind?" he asked Marty, but he shook his head. He never cared much for politics; the only office-holders that interested him were dead ones who'd had the foresight to preserve their voices for Tom Edison around the turn of the century.

Herb glanced impatiently at his watch. "Our luck

## My Son, the Druggist

she's probably at the end of a block-long line." Betty expressed a wish that Carol might not prove to be a chain smoker. "With all the windows closed, I'm liable to get sick."

Marty scarcely heard. Thinking of Loretta reminded him of her late neighbor, Mrs. Fenimore. His preoccupation lasted through the remainder of the ride, as well as the film, which he'd already seen.

Afterwards, the plan was to drive to Herb's for snacks and drinks, the idea being to permit Marty to get to know Carol better. But she scotched the scheme by insisting on going to a club on Seventy-ninth.

"I hear it swings," she said casually, lighting her sixth cigarette from the smoldering remains of the fifth.

Herb Adelstein tried to talk her out of it, but received no support from Marty, who was still lost in thought. Carol finally got her way.

Seventy-five minutes later, Bill Finney, seated naked on his bed, looked up from a morose contemplation of his navel.

"Lieber Herr Gold!" he exclaimed, bowing with difficulty in his Buddha-like position, "what brings you back home so soon? By now, I'd thought you'd be engaged in some unmentionable pursuit."

"The evening didn't pan out," said Marty, flopping onto a frayed, bulging beige armchair.

"Condolences, O Compounder of Poultices! What transpired?"

"My date picked up somebody else." Marty took off his shoes.

Bill Finney's eyebrows shot up in astonishment.

"Zounds, sirrah, shall she 'scape whipping?"

Marty stretched out his stockinged feet and yawned. "She made us go to The Sleave Joint. Somebody she'd met the other night there grabbed her again. Herbie said it didn't surprise him, the way she behaved." He sighed. "I don't know. Why should I give a damn?"

"Because," said his roommate, "she humiliated you before friends."

"I guess you're right." Marty shook his head. "I don't understand it. Most of my friends are already hooked, but me, I can't even find a girl who halfway fits the requirements."

"I don't pretend to have much experience in this quarter," Finney said, patting his ample stomach, "not with this spare tire interfering with my love life. However, I might venture to remark, first of all, that nowadays, few women like to be called 'girls' . . ."

Marty waved a hand impatiently. "Hard to break old speech habits."

"—and second of all, Herr Martin, what are these precious requirements your hypothetical Aphrodite must meet?"

"If I *knew*, I'd be a lot better off. Carol has my parents' approval, and I thought she was pretty terrific at first myself, but now—" He gestured vaguely, unable to find the right words.

Bill Finney nodded. "I know whereof you speak. If you've ever seen the movie of *A Taste of Honey*, you may remember Rita Tushingham, who played the lead. She was plain and unappealing at first, but after you got inside her head, she became more and more beautiful. Objectively."

"Yeah," Marty sighed, "and Carol's growing uglier by

the minute." He regarded his hands as he continued, half to himself. "Then, the other day, another . . ." He paused.

"Hm?"

*Should I tell him about it?*

"The other day?" the actor prompted.

Marty described the interlude with Loretta Hamilton. When he was finished, Bill Finney raised his ponderous bulk and lumbered into the kitchen. "You need a drink, my good apothecary."

"Nothing fancy, Bill," Marty requested, somewhat apprehensively, but his plea went unheeded. His roommate concocted a strange, medium-vile brew which he called hot buttered rum, which it wasn't.

When he was seated once more, still naked, still looking like an oversized Ho-Toy figurine, Bill Finney resumed the conversation.

"This Ms. Hamilton," he rumbled, pausing to sip from a glass full of adulterated rum, "sounds decent enough. I don't see what objections you have to what seems to me to have been a pleasant interlude."

"My father would go right through the roof if he heard," Marty replied, taking a taste of his drink and grimacing.

"So who's going to tell him? You? Me?"

"Bill, there's no need to. In my mind, he's already shouting at me."

"That," said Finney, "is just your hyperstimulated Jewish conscience. You have to learn to cauterize it."

"But, damn it, Bill, if I hadn't been fooling around with her, I might have saved a life!"

His roommate put down his drink and regarded him

with narrowed eyes. "It appears, Guidman Gold, that you left something out in your recounting . . ."

"One of our oldest customers, Mrs. Fenimore, called up and wanted me to stop over, she wasn't feeling well. We got too busy and I forgot. Then, after work, I remembered and walked over to her place . . . and that's where I met Loretta."

"Mm-hm. And you neglected your errand of mercy."

"Practically. I *did* ring Mrs. Fenimore's doorbell before I left, but there was no answer."

"And what happened to her?"

"Her son found her body."

"Heart attack?"

"Partially. But it was mainly caused by an allergic reaction. She couldn't take a substance called phenylbutazone, but somehow she must have ingested some pills with it in them, from what I understand. I don't know all the details."

"How much would she have to swallow? I thought it takes a lot of allergenic to cause death."

"It varies tremendously from person to person. A mild reaction might be itching, hives, difficulty in swallowing. But a big dosage, I would imagine—"

"Imagine? Don't you know?"

"I can't keep track of it *all* in my head," Marty said, getting up and going to a brick-and-cinderblock bookcase in the corner. "Wait a minute." He extracted a large blue book and a smaller tan one and flipped through them till he found what he was seeking.

"What are those?" Bill Finney asked.

"PDR. *Physician's Desk Reference.* The other's a compendium of toxic reactions to drugs. I'm looking up the stuff, Butazolidin."

"What's that?"

"Butazolidin Alka. The brand name of the drug that was originally prescribed for her."

"She was *taking* it?"

"No, she had an allergic reaction from the drug. About a year ago she suffered a severe attack, and that put the capper on her ever going near the stuff again. Or it should have." Marty ran his finger down the page, rapidly reading the manufacturer's contraindications. "Yeah, look at this. There's practically two pages of warnings, all sorts of problems this stuff can cause."

"Render it in English," Finney said, finishing his rum travesty.

"Well, you can have a whole range of symptoms, from skin itch on up in a case like hers to fatal shock, heart failure."

"How much does it take to kill?"

"No constant amount. When someone is as allergic to a substance as she was to Butazolidin, a minute quantity can be fatal."

"Then stop tormenting yourself. If she called hours earlier, she was surely dead by the time you were fooling around with the Hamilton person."

Marty walked to the kitchen and poured out the rest of his drink. "Some comfort, Bill," he grumbled. "That only tells me I should have gone over there right away."

"If the lady had any sense, she would have called a doctor!"

*That's what she thought she was doing.*

"She tried her physician, but he couldn't be reached,

and Bill, to her I was, anyway, doctor, nurse and confessor, all in one. I should've been there."

"My friend," the other said seriously, "don't play God. If there was one, *he* would have been there . . ."

Marty ignored the remark and got ready for bed.

Deputy Inspector Abner T. Chubb, referred to surreptitiously as Chubby L'il Abner by his colleagues, styled himself a pragmatist, a rationalist, an illusionless New York policeman whose duty it was to regard every citizen as potentially corrupt. But since he was really a soured romanticist, his cynicism was rooted not in conviction, but in a deep fear that his basic trust in humanity would be shattered if reindulged. The last thing the inspector really wanted was confirmation of his hardheaded philosophy, but his profession provided it every day. He was therefore a deeply disturbed man.

Privately, Chubb was soft-spoken, hesitant to voice his opinions. Publicly, he was authoritarian and eternally suspicious, occasionally even pugnacious. In keeping with his erroneous self-image of himself as a policeman, he literally presented a stern face to those culprits and felons he wished he did not have to deal with constantly. His forbidding posture was aided by circumstance, since his head was shaped like a bullet, with about as much hair, and his features were puffy, protrusive and rather cruel-looking.

His narrow, piggy eyes regarded Marty Gold. He rather liked the young man, so, as a matter of policy, he forced himself to distrust him.

*Big-headed,* Chubb thought, cataloguing the young pharmacist in the computer he pretended was in his head. *Ought to plaster down the hair that sticks up.*

*About five feet seven, a hundred and forty-five pounds. Stocky. Swarthy. Why doesn't he look straight at me?*

"Go ahead in," the policeman suggested. "Everything's been picked over, you won't disturb anything."

He waited while the fat pharmacist entered first, followed by Marty Gold. Then Chubb stepped through the door and closed it.

*Typical West Side flat,* Chubb reflected, going over the apartment for the tenth time in his mind. *Ceilings maybe ten point five feet high. Living room size of a European salon. Kitchen: tiny, space-wasting. Bedroom, thirty by thirty, immense. Carpeting, dark green, deep pile, wall to wall, fairly new. Furniture elegant, not new, polished wood, mirror-gloss surface, but chips and nicks from intermediate generations.*

Chubb pointed to a frail mahogany table that held the telephone. "Found her body next to that," he said. "Figure she must've been calling, trying to get help."

Marty Gold, feeling nervous, looked away. The inspector noticed; the flesh at his temples puckered as he narrowed his eyes.

*Better question him later . . .*

"The bathroom's over this way. Take a look. She had her own drugstore in there," said Chubb.

Spector handed the record book containing the Fenimore file to his assistant, then walked into the toilet facility and yanked open the medicine chest.

"Chrissake!" he swore beneath his breath.

Four shelves of closely packed containers of pills, tubes of salves and balms, medicines to assuage aches, reduce pain, induce slumber, retard nausea, soothe grumbling stomachs, stimulate laggard bile production, oxydize histamines—the accumulated dross of a lifetime of bodily anomaly and protest.

"Gonna take a good hour to check this stuff all out," Spector said.

Since the room was too small to accommodate all three comfortably, Chubb stood in the doorway watching their progress.

*Fenimore must've been a scrub bug,* the inspector mused. *Sparkling. Pristine. No dirt, not even between the tile cracks. Must've gone at them with toothpicks.* He was reminded of his own fanatically neat parent.

Eighty minutes of painstaking cataloguing. Spector would pick up a vial, read the prescription number to Marty Gold, who looked it up in the medical record to check the original date and number of refills. Spector would set it aside and go on to the next substance. At last, they were done. The two pharmacists wearily flopped on the living-room sofa; the slipcover crackled beneath their accumulated weight.

Inspector Chubb selected a tawny armchair and lowered himself into it, extending his feet to get comfortable. He took out his pen and black notebook.

"What's the story?" he asked Spector.

"I have to preface this with a confession," the old man said, tugging at his mustache. "By law, we're supposed to require a prescription blank each time, unless the physician specifically stipulates repeats, and even then, there's a limit to the number."

"Why are you telling me this?" asked Chubb. "I'm not from the FDA."

"Some of our old-timers like Mrs. Fonimore drive us up the wall asking for stuff over the refill limit, and if you make them go back to the doctor, they bang your ear and sometimes take their business somewhere else, which means they forget about their bills. Some of them don't want to be bothered making a trip to the doctor just to get a piece of paper. Others can't afford to pay the doctor so often. So if it's not dangerous and heavily controlled, we fudge sometimes and let them have an extra refill or two. Mrs. Fenimore's medicine cabinet is full of things that were issued without a covering prescription."

"She usually forgot to bring in the pill bottle, even when it had a few legitimate repeats on it," Marty Gold added. "I'd have to look in her file for the original strength and dosage. The last time I saw her, in fact, she wanted some Darvon for bursitis pain—"

Chubb held up a finger to stop Marty. "You're saying this was the last meeting you had with the deceased?"

Marty nodded.

*How come he didn't tell me that before?*

"This Darvon," Chubb asked, "I don't suppose it could cause a similar reaction to—"

"Phenylbutazone," Spector snorted. "Not a chance!"

"All right, go on, Mr. Gold," said Chubb. "She arrived in the store for some medicine for her bursitis. And then . . . ?"

"She didn't have the old pill bottle with her, so I had to look it up. When I saw how old the original prescription was, it crossed my mind to tell her to go to Dr. Paul for an update, but then it got too busy, and I figured the hell with it, I'd ask her next time."

Chubb's manner was elaborately casual as he asked the next question. "I wonder, is there any chance that when

## My Son, the Druggist

the Darvon was being prepared, some of the other stuff might have happened in by accident?"

Spector vigorously shook his head. "The days of pill rolling are just about over, Inspector. Couple of years ago, somebody figured out only two point five per cent of all prescriptions written in this country are compounded by the druggist. Most pills are premade and shipped by the manufacturers, and our job is chiefly to find the right bottle and count the capsules. No, the only medicine in that cabinet containing the allergenic is the Butazolidin Alka."

"The original medicine prescribed by Dr. Paul."

"Yes," Spector said. "It's the only such prescription we have on record for Mrs. Fenimore, as it should be."

"I checked with your Dr. Paul," the inspector said, "he only wrote the one prescription."

"Like I said, that's how it should be," Spector reiterated. "It's carefully controlled. Can't be refilled. The physician writes an order for maybe twenty-four or thirty pills and sees how the patient reacts to them."

"By the way," the policeman said casually, "I gather you and Doc Paul aren't on the best of terms?"

Spector made a rude sound.

"Yes, you did that yesterday, but would you like to tell me why?"

"It's an old story," the pharmacist stated. "He always thought he was God's gift to medicine, the man who can do no wrong. Except I gave 'im a big hassle several years ago about a prescription he wrote. I said the dosage was too strong, it would kill the patient. He argued with me, told me off on the phone and in person, in front of my customers. But I was right."

"What'd he do wrong?"

"He just got off the boat from the Old Country, and forgot and wrote down the strength in metric terms, instead of ounces. The figure was enormous, might've felled a horse . . . and now, Fenimore's dead. He should never have prescribed a dangerous drug like that for a woman with such a bad medical history."

Chubb nodded. "All right. Let's get back to the bottle of medicine in the cabinet. Is *it* the right dosage?"

"Any dosage could've killed her," Marty volunteered.

Spector answered. "For bursitis, recommended dosage can be from three hundred to six hundred milligrams in three or four equal doses. Paul prescribed five hundred milligrams three times a day. That fits the suggested regimen, but it's high, which proves he's a—"

"Never mind." Chubb waved him down. "You sold her what? Two dozen pills?"

"Uh-huh."

"And did you notice how many are left in the bottle?"

"Seventeen," said Marty.

"Correct." Chubb made an entry in his notebook. "How do you account for that number remaining?"

The young man shrugged. "It's a carefully controlled substance, and she had a fast allergic reaction, Lou tells me. So we can reasonably assume these are the only Butazolidins she ever had prescribed for her by any doctor. Now let's see . . . she takes her first dosage practically a year ago. Five pills. She gets damn sick and has to be hospitalized. Remainder: nineteen pills."

"Which leaves two unaccounted for," Spector murmured.

Chubb nodded. "What are the possibilities? Might she

have taken more than the five prescribed for her at the initial dosage?"

"Negative," Marty replied. "She wouldn't have O.D.'d either by accident or deliberately, and she wouldn't have taken a drug that had been discontinued for her. Whatever a doctor or a druggist told her was gospel, that's how she was."

"She might've played doctor herself," Spector observed, tapping his fingers nervously against his lip, flicking the hairs of his mustache against the grain. "Maybe prescribed them for one of her relatives."

Marty doggedly shook his head. "Lou, Lou, you know better. Doctors were gods to her. She wouldn't have set herself on the same level. It would've been practically sacrilege."

Chubb closed his notebook. "Then you definitely think the two missing pills were taken by Mrs. Fenimore to commit suicide?"

"Well, they *are* gone," Marty said. "Where else did they go?" He shuddered. "It just doesn't make sense, though, why she'd pick such an awful way to die."

The inspector gestured impatiently. "What are you saying, Mr. Gold? That it was *not* suicide?"

"Well . . . not really. She just wasn't the type. But still, the two pills *are* missing. How else could the drug enter her system?"

The policeman regarded him curiously. *Is he playing dumb?*

"Maybe," said Spector, "she swallowed Butazolidin thinking it was Darvon."

"Lou, the colors aren't the same, the shapes are noticeably differentiated. And she didn't have weak eyes."

"How do you know that?"

"She never complained particularly about her vision. And believe me, I heard all her kvetches."

"Gentlemen," Chubb said quietly, "there *is* another way to account for the missing pills . . ."

The druggists looked at him. Neither of them spoke.

"You see," Chubb continued, "there's a psychological oddity about the suicide theory. If she was so slavish about always following the doctor's instructions, then, since she took a first dose of the drug, the dose that laid her up . . . well . . ."

Marty slapped his forehead with his open palm. "Of course! If she were going to kill herself, she probably would have automatically taken five pills, not just two!"

"Possibly, possibly," said Chubb, turning to a fresh page in his notebook. "And now, Mr. Spector, you will have to excuse us for a while. I have some questions to ask Mr. Gold."

"Aah, cops're no damn good in this city," Spector complained as he counted pills from the tray. "Two weeks ago I'm in Times Square, three guys come up to me at different times, ask me right there if I want to buy joints. But I go to a pretzel vendor to get a snack, and this cop stops me because the guy doesn't have a license!"

Etta Spector—who was busy with the monthly billing (it was handled by a computer service, but she insisted on verifying the machine's arithmetic)—looked up at her husband and nodded. "Remember from Harry Kleinman?" she asked. "A hooligan sticks a gun in his side, stands behind the counter with him next to the cash register and smiles, like he worked there. The customers don't know, they don't see the gun. Everything that goes into the cash drawer goes into his pocket. Meantime, the cops are riding past, they don't even look in!"

Spector nodded wisely. "That's why I keep pictures posted of all the druggists and even the kid in the cellar. I want the cops to know who belongs behind the counter, who doesn't. Only they never stop in to learn."

"They get shifted around too much from neighborhood to neighborhood," the relief pharmacist, Joe Rubens, murmured. He was a small, sour man who rarely spoke.

"There was Hermie Samuels," Spector continued. "Built himself a special room, in case of robbers. All he had to do was step in it, the door was bulletproof . ."

They had been discussing the investigation all morning. Eventually the talk drifted away from death and focused on other crimes involving pharmacies. Spector ridiculed the old narcotics act that required such drugs to be kept locked up. "We might as well have hung up a sign saying, 'Thieves, right this way to the stuff.'"

Marty did not participate. The day was a gray blur to him. He would have liked to talk to Herb, but it was his day off, and Joe Rubens was not the sort to invite confidences. He went through his duties in a daze, and thought about Mrs. Fenimore.

*Wish I could talk to her. I miss her.*

Loretta Hamilton came in at one-thirty, dressed for church. She made a few minor purchases, brought them to Marty to ring up and leaned close.

"Stop over when you're through," she suggested. "It'll be lonely at my place this afternoon."

She had to repeat herself. He wasn't listening.

"Aah, I'd like to," he hedged, "but I can't. Family stuff, y'know?"

She pretended to pout. "I think you don't want to see me again, Marty."

He glanced nervously at the Old Lady staring suspiciously at the two of them. "Listen, Mrs. Hamilton—"

"Loretta."

"Loretta, I can't talk now. I'll try to stop by later this week."

"That," she said, smiling as she collected her change, "is a *promise* . . ."

As she went out the door, the Old Lady nodded her head knowingly, disapprovingly. Marty pretended not to notice.

*That's all I need now, to be hanging around the Fenimore place.*

## My Son, the Druggist

Inspector Chubb's questions had made Marty uneasy. He'd told him all he could remember about the last time he'd seen her alive, plus the morning of the phone call, but his recounting of the visit late in the day excluded his stopover at Loretta Hamilton's apartment.

*It's nobody's business.*

The workday ended. He had to spend the evening with his parents because it was the last day their houseguests would be there. Carol looked spectacular, as usual, but he confined his conversation with her to polite generalities. His mother noticed the coolness of his manner and took him aside.

"Marty," she asked, her mouth twisting in her customary nervous moue, "what's wrong you're not talking to Carol?"

"I'm talking, I'm talking."

"Like your father whispers, that's how you're talking. What kind of behavior is this, I'm asking you? You keep her out all night two nights, God knows what the two of you were doing,—because *I'd* rather *not* know—and this, *this* is the result? 'Thanks, but go back to Philadelphia, I'm finished with you?'"

"Ma . . ."

"Don't 'Ma' me, that's how it is!"

"That's *not* the way it is."

"Then you tell me, Marty, *you* tell me how it is."

*What's the use?*

He gestured hopelessly. "It's not worth getting aggravated about."

*Let it go. Otherwise, she'll complain to Carol, Tessie will answer back, before you know it Dud'll be hollering. I'd rather stay the villain.*

Ida Gold was not through with the discussion, but Marty refused to answer back; failing to get any feedback, she began to falter. Just then, her husband interrupted.

"Ida," he declared in his normal *fff* speaking voice, "leave off hocking him whatever you're hocking and get me a soda." He gestured for his son to come near and then, in a tone he thought private, asked, "What's the matter, Marty, you're not shmootzing all over the Bazoom Kid?"

It was a long and trying evening for Marty Gold.

He finally begged off at eleven and went straight home. Bill Finney was out, but there was a message in his handwriting:

CALL MR. BERKOWITZ, ANY HOUR. IMPORTANT. 719-5503.

Marty stared curiously at the brief note.
*Who the hell is Mr. Berkowitz?*

"Mr. Gold," a gruff voice said, "I'm sorry to disturb you on a Sunday, but it can't wait. I represent the late Mrs. Fenimore."

For no good reason, Marty's stomach began to knot.

"The family doesn't want to wait any longer than necessary," the attorney explained, "so the will is being read tomorrow, right after the service. About noon, I'd imagine."

"Mr. Berkowitz, how does this concern me?"

"I felt you would want to be there."

"For the funeral?"

"For the reading of the will. You're in it."

Little life exists on the 500 block of East Eighty-first Street, especially in the middle of the north side where Spencer & Malin Funeral Parlors is situated. Residents leave in the morning for more populous sections of Manhattan and shut themselves up in the evening behind safety-chained doors. The principal sentience, other than migratory traffic, dwells in the stunted trees, screened by barbed wire to protect them from vandalism and nuisance. Once, Harry Malin, junior partner of the mortuary, offered to uproot the scraggly greenery and replace it with weeping willows, but the block association sarcastically demurred.

Marty Gold and his roommate, Bill Finney, hurried along the street toward the modest reconverted brownstone that housed the undertaking establishment. It was a few minutes before noon.

"I feel like a fool," Finney said, puffing for breath. "I don't have any business here." He was particularly uncomfortable because Marty insisted on his donning his sole dress suit—a garment that had exhausted Finney's tailor.

"Keep me company," Marty pleaded. "I'll feel better if I don't have to go in there alone."

"But *you* were invited."

"The family might have other ideas about my coming."

"Then why didn't you stay home? It's your day off, you could be at the library. You could meet the attorney privately."

"True."

"So why did you come?"

Marty shrugged. "Damned if *I* know."

*Oh? It couldn't by any chance be that you want to see Melinda again?*

They stepped along the dark-green runner leading up to the canopied front door. Before Marty could reach for the handle, it turned and Inspector Abner Chubb emerged from the portal. When he saw Marty, his beady eyes widened a trifle, then narrowed.

"What are you doing here?" he asked.

"The lawyer asked me to come to the reading of Mrs. Fenimore's will."

"Oh?" The policeman regarded him casually, politely, as if his presence was of little consequence. He extracted a thin cigar and lit it. "The funeral is still going strong. It'll be another couple minutes before they're ready to read the will."

Marty nodded and tried to get to the doorway, but the policeman blocked the way. As he began to edge past, Chubb put a restraining hand on his arm. The touch was gentle enough, but Marty sensed an abrupt change in the other's manner.

"I want to ask you a few questions," said Chubb.

Marty was puzzled. "I thought I told you everything."

"Not quite. I spoke with the doorman of Mrs. Fenimore's building. He says he let you in Friday afternoon to see her, but you never came out."

*Uh-oh, so that's it . . .*

"I believe you told me, Mr. Gold, that you approached her door, rang the bell, got no answer, and left?"

"Yes."

"How did you leave the building? By the basement?"

"No," Marty replied, shaking his head. "I went out the front way. Cholly was busy sweeping and didn't see me."

Chubb nodded. "Possibly. However, he claims he didn't quit his post by the front doorway for well over an hour after you took the elevator. It was just after work. Too many people were coming home for him to leave the door unattended."

Marty said nothing.

Bill Finney nudged him. "Marty, I suggest—"

"Yeah," the other nodded, with a sigh. "All right, I left quite a while later, Inspector. Maybe an hour, hour and a half, I don't remember precisely."

"What were you doing in her apartment all that time?"

"I wasn't in her apartment! I was visiting a . . . friend."

"Who?"

"I'd rather not say."

The taut skin of Chubb's forehead and scalp colored a delicate scarlet. "Mr. Gold, in case it hasn't struck you yet, you are involved in an investigation of possible—"

*"But it's personal!"*

Before the policeman could argue, Bill Finney intervened. "He was enjoying the favors of some wench named Loretta Hamilton."

"Thanks a lot!" Marty groaned.

Chubb's notebook was out. "Her apartment number?"

"Same floor as Mrs. Fenimore. I don't know the letter."

"And after you left?"

"I tried the Fenimore bell, then went home and changed to go to Friday night services with my family."

"I can verify the time he arrived home," his roommate said.

"I'll expect you to," the inspector replied curtly. "All

right now, Gold—" (He always dropped the "Mister" when he slid into his Class Three Intimidating Style, for allegedly-innocent-but-suspicious citizens.) "All right, Gold, tell me what you were doing the night before she died."

"On Thanksgiving? Why?"

"Because I'm asking, that's why!"

"I spent the evening with my parents. They had guests in from Philadelphia, and I came for dinner."

"Were you there *all* night?"

Marty hesitated.

"Well? I'd like an answer!"

"After dinner, I went for a walk with one of my parents' guests—"

"Name?"

*Jesus Christ! He'll call her in Philly, she'll blab to her aunt, she'll talk to my—*

"I said, *name?*"

"Carol Blum."

"Address?"

"I don't know."

"And the two of you just went for a walk?"

"No," Marty said, hardly above a mumble, "we went out to a club, stayed there practically the whole night."

"*Which* club?"

"The Sleave Joint on Seventy-ninth East."

Chubb nodded, then snapped his notebook shut.

"Is that all?" Marty asked apprehensively.

"For now," the inspector said, and went inside.

Marty exchanged a worried glance with his roommate and followed in the detective's wake.

When Marty Gold and Bill Finney entered the hushed anteroom, they found Lukas Fenimore by himself. Chubb was in the hallway making a phone call, and the others were still in the chapel.

It turned out that Lukas and Bill knew one another slightly, having both acted in an Equity showcase several months earlier. They exchanged desultory greetings, but the mourner barely acknowledged Marty's presence.

Lukas was rather tall and so thin that he seemed even lankier. His hair resembled straw, both in hue and in its tousled appearance, and his blue eyes shone with an odd light. His hands could not keep still; if they were not fidgeting with each other, unconsciously forming church steeples, they were busy rummaging in coat or trouser pockets, extracting pencils to rap against knuckles, keys to rattle upon the crystal of his watch, coins to roll between forefingers and thumbs.

"I'm surprised," said Bill Finney, "that you've decided to hear the will before going to the cemetery. Isn't that a bit odd?"

"Anything to accommodate my glorious brother-in-law," Lukas said sourly, passing a quarter from one hand to the other. "He has rounds at Polyclinic, so he can't run out to the cemetery. And my sister wants to catch a flight home."

"Your sister?" Marty asked. "Melinda?"

Lukas shot him an unfriendly look. "I have three sisters." He volunteered no further information.

Marty nudged his roommate and they walked across the room to some chairs not too near Lukas.

"See?" Marty whispered. "I told you I wouldn't be especially welcome. At least you know him under a different set of circumstances."

"I admit," Bill Finney stated, "that I seem to be of some use as a buffer." He pointed to the opening door. "But who's this? One of the sisters?"

"Yes," Marty replied. "That's Melinda."

She was clearly agitated. The emotion actually enhanced her already attractive features. She was petite and delicate, and her face might have served as a model for cameo portraiture. High cheekbones, eyebrows delicately arched, a small, straight nose and pale lips slightly parted. Her eyes were a faded shade of green, with a childlike luster that Marty found appealing. He thought he sensed a vulnerability, a yearning in them.

She walked past Lukas without speaking, evidently preoccupied. Then she saw Marty looking at her and her troubles momentarily loosened their hold and the frown left her face. She stared at him, perplexed.

"Contact lenses," Bill Finney remarked.

"How do you know?" Marty whispered.

"I've seen that melting look in women's eyes before. It speaks of unexpressed tender feelings—when it really has to do with the refraction of light from the bits of plastic. Manufactured mystery. Behind them, they're empty-headed trolls."

"You're a cynic."

"It's less painful than the romantic agony."

Melinda approached. Marty stood up, feeling awkward. *What the hell should I say? I'll make a fool—*

"Don't I know you from somewhere?" she asked. She had a light voice, pleasant to the ear but difficult to hear; she rarely spoke very loud.

"I'm Marty Gold," he said, wishing he'd remembered to comb his hair before entering the room. He was certain the damned cowlick was sticking up again.

*And she hardly even remembers me.*

"Marty Gold?" she repeated, still puzzled.

"We went to Stahley High together."

Her eyes widened in recognition. "Ye-es! Of course! I never knew your last name. But you used to sit behind me in assembly hall and I always heard you talking about old records and silent-film comedies. You were a year ahead of me, I think."

Marty was surprised and pleased. "You remember all that?"

A rueful smile touched her lips and was gone. It reminded Marty of one of her mother's expressions. "Once," Melinda said, "I hoped you might ask me to go to one of those screenings. But I was too shy and you never noticed me." She shrugged. "It's so long ago, it's strange to think how important it was then. And today, I couldn't even place who you are. Funny how things change."

Feeling peculiar and elated all at once, as if he were mildly high on gunpowder tea, Marty groped for something intelligent to say. "I guess we're both out of context here."

"Why *are* you here?" she asked. "Did you know my mother?"

"Yes. She was a regular customer where I work."

"Where's that?"

"Spector's pharmacy on Eighty-sixth, near Amsterdam."

"You're a pharmacist?" Lukas interrupted from across the room. Marty nodded in reply, and the young man demanded, "Did you sell my mother the stuff that killed her?"

Melinda stared at her brother in shocked silence. She turned to apologize to Marty, but the door opened and a man in an impeccably tailored tan suit entered and walked over to her. He was young and very good-looking, but though his mouth wore a slight smile, his eyes did not.

*Talk about recognizing faces . . . where the hell have I seen him before?*

"Lin," the newcomer said in a calm voice, "why did you leave the chapel?"

"To be alone," she answered curtly.

"Will you look at me, please, when I talk to you?" His voice was even, extremely controlled, but the slight accentuation of the pronounced consonants suggested inner tension.

Marty instantly disliked him.

"This is my husband," Melinda told Marty, "Steven Rush. Steve, this is an old school friend, Marty Gold."

Rush barely acknowledged Marty's presence with a nod.

*Steve Rush. That's why he seems familiar.*

Marty had been seeing his face plastered on billboards all over the West Side. He was an attorney running for the position of representative to the State Assembly, and there was reason to believe he would win the election.

*If only for his pretty punim.*

Rush confronted his wife, his hands by his side, thumbs

and forefingers pressed lightly together to lend poise—a trick taught him by his PR agent.

"I asked why you left," he repeated.

She made him a mock curtsy. "I don't wish to tarnish your image, Your Honor. Or is it your worship? I forget."

"Knock it off!" he snapped. It was the first time his voice lost its deceptive serenity.

"I suppose you think I didn't notice your solicitous concern!" she retorted.

He glanced uneasily at Marty and the fat stranger sitting behind him. "All right, that's enough, Lin. Spare me your paranoia today at least."

He walked to the other side of the room before she could reply. Rush withdrew a mirror and comb from his pocket and corrected the way the front of his hair fell.

Marty watched him with disdain. *Even the curl over his right eye is deliberate. Must've read Ian Fleming.*

Several people entered the room. A powerfully built gentleman with gray hair and tortoiseshell glasses had a briefcase under his arm. Marty assumed he was the attorney, Reuben Berkowitz, and was correct. Abner Chubb took up a seat near the door and regarded the others without affection. His eye caught Marty's, and the pharmacist glanced away nervously.

A short, fortyish man with a shape like a barrel, stubby arms and hands and a spiky beard the size and shape of an Amish farmer's held the door open while the two remaining daughters of the deceased swept into the room.

The first was a tall, voluptuous honey-blonde with soft skin and hard eyes. She took a chair next to Melinda. The second, older woman was matronly and had an authoritarian air as she walked to the front of the room and sat next to the table on which the attorney had placed his papers. The bearded man shut the door and joined the latter woman, his wife.

Counselor Reuben Berkowitz was immaculate in white linen shirt, charcoal-gray flannel, and a tie whose pallidity could not possibly offend the eye of the bereaved. His expression was somber as he stroked his chin, as if seeking some appropriate doleful phrase to open his remarks. He actually was wondering whether he might get a closer shave with a rotary-head Norelco.

He nodded at the bearded man and his spouse. "Dr. and Mrs. McKaye asked that I be brief," the lawyer began. "If no one has an objection, I'll give you the gist of the will without the legal terminology." He paused, noted no protest, then continued. "My late client was in the habit of frequently altering the terms of her estate's disposal. The will now in my possession is fairly recent, but she phoned me a few days ago to make an appointment, so I presume she might have further modified the document. However, she did not live to keep that appointment."

"Keep it short," Lukas murmured, fidgeting in his chair. Marty glanced over at him.

*Christ, doesn't he ever sit still? What would Mom call it? "He twists around like he's got shpilkas!"*

"I only mention the last phone call," Berkowitz said, "because I wanted to make sure that you all understand that any recent promises of Mrs. Fenimore's concerning her estate were probably not effected." He picked up a pencil and placed its point upon a sheet of paper next to the first of several items he wished to mention. "Now,

*My Son, the Druggist*

then, as to the exact terms and bequests . . . there are many involving charitable organizations, including Dr. McKaye's private clinic. The administration of these bequests is all reserved to the doctor."

"Naturally," Regina McKaye declared. She waited for any of her family to offer a contrary opinion, but they did not. She dismissed the matter with a short decisive nod.

"Dr. and Mrs. McKaye," the attorney continued, crossing out a line on the paper, "have also been detailed to take care of the securities and trusts in the Fenimore portfolio. Out of the proceeds, they are to act in concert with myself to provide a fair fixed income to Ms. Brand."

"How much?" the honey-blonde asked softly.

"Dinah, this is not the time to ask," Regina declared.

"*How much?*"

"The income was fixed by your mother on a sliding scale," the attorney replied. "The plateaus are governed by two conditions she stipulated you meet."

"What are they?"

Berkowitz avoided her eyes. "I think it best to discuss them in private."

The blond woman nodded but did not speak. She looked down at her hands clasped in her lap and did not look up again.

The attorney consulted his notes. "The dividends from securities and trusts not specifically spoken for go to various charities that my client supported. Incidentally, there is a fee to be paid Dr. and Mrs. McKaye and to myself for administration of these matters. Otherwise, though, Mrs. Fenimore maintains in her will that her eldest daughter and her husband are independently wealthy and require no additional funds. None have been allocated to them."

Regina McKaye stared at the attorney in mild surprise, and might have spoken, but her husband tapped her as he leaned his head close and muttered so only she could hear. She nodded and held her tongue.

"The remainder of the estate," Berkowitz continued, "consists of three specific bequests. Fifty thousand dollars to be paid over a period of five years to Melinda Fenimore Rush."

Marty glanced at her. She remained silent, and the only reaction he noted was a slight reddening of her cheeks, as if she'd heard something faintly off-color.

"An amount of ten thousand dollars, plus an additional stipend to defray the taxes on the base figure, is to be paid Mr. Martin Gold so that, in my client's words, 'he may pursue his true profession.'"

"What in hell does that mean?" Lukas asked.

"I suggest you take it up with Mr. Gold," the lawyer remarked dryly.

"All right, never mind. What about me?"

"Lukas, hush!" Melinda said quietly. Marty wondered whether she was the only one in the family to care about her mother's death.

"What about *me?*" Lukas insisted, nervously rattling his keys.

Berkowitz answered him. "The will earmarks an amount equal to that bestowed on Mrs. Rush." He checked off the final entry on his list.

Marty wondered about the odd expression on Lukas' face.

*Not so much pleased as relieved.*

"Do I get it all at once, or is it distributed over a couple of years, like my sister's?"

The attorney appeared embarrassed. "Mr. Fenimore, I'm afraid it doesn't come at all until you are thirty-five."

Lukas stiffened. The color drained from his cheeks.

"Your mother appointed me your financial guardian," said Berkowitz. "I am to see you have enough capital to live on, but otherwise, there are extremely rigid limits, I'm afraid."

"*You're* afraid?" Lukas snapped, a wild look in his eye. He pointed to Marty Gold. "You mean *he* gets ten thousand, just like that, and she gives her son *nothing?*"

The counselor shrugged, at a loss for words.

"Lukas, stop making a nuisance of yourself," said Regina.

He rose, glowering at her, tried to speak, then gave it up and hurried out of the room. Melinda rose and followed.

She returned a moment later.

"I can't calm him down."

"So let him be angry," Regina yawned. "We're all used to his tantrums."

"But he's liable to hurt someone," Melinda protested. "Or himself."

No one spoke.

"*Please!* Someone go after him!"

Marty Gold nudged Bill Finney. They rose.

Melinda gave them a grateful smile.

When they came out of the funeral parlor, Lukas was halfway up the block, walking toward Second Avenue. They hurried.

Neither noticed Inspector Chubb stick his head out the front door and signal to someone across the street. He pointed in Marty's direction.

It was a nondescript corner tavern, and the people in it at that time of day were deadly serious about getting drunk. The only sound was the clink of glassware.

Lukas had just downed a double Dewar's and was chasing it with a pint of Michelob when Marty and Bill Finney slid into his booth and sat opposite him.

"What the hell are *you* doing here?" Lukas asked, glaring.

"Your sister wanted someone to make sure you were all right," Marty replied.

"I wonder which sister that could be?" Lukas mused, heavily sarcastic. "All right, you see I'm okay, now butt out."

"Look, it's none of my business," Marty began, and got no further.

"You're damn right it isn't! Who the hell are you, anyway? How long did you have to suck up to my old lady to—"

"Jesus Christ!" Marty exclaimed. "She's dead! Don't you care about that at all?"

Lukas said nothing for a time. He drained the rest of his beer, held up his hand for a refill and waited till he got it before replying.

"There was a time," he said softly, "when I would have been able to feel sorry about her, but that was two years ago. She made me get out of the house, and ever since, nothing's been right. Christ, I cried then, but she threw me out. *That's* when she died." He downed the scotch in two convulsive swallows, wiped his lips roughly with the back of a finger.

Bill Finney put a hand on Marty Gold's arm, restraining him from further comment.

"Luke," Finney said, "I don't wish to be tactless, but may I ask a question?"

The other nodded. "Go ahead."

"Are you still on the stuff?"

Lukas evaded his eyes. "That's not the problem."

"Isn't it?"

"No. I have . . . debts."

Bill Finney exhaled like an asthmatic walrus. "How much? Or is it more important to ask to whom?"

"You don't want to hear the answer."

Bill Finney grimly shook his head.

Marty Gold looked from one to the other, baffled.

"Do you mind telling me what you're both talking about?"

His roommate answered him. "There is a substratum of particularly virulent virus that preys on impecunious theater people, making loans at usurious interest rates. Or favors. I suspect Lukas here is the host body for one." He peered inquisitively at the other, and Lukas nodded.

"I blew a couple thousand in a poker game, and I had no choice about paying it back fast. It was either pay it, or get my thumbs broken."

"Why didn't you go straight to one of your relatives?" Bill Finney asked.

"Fat chance," Lukas sneered. "Melinda doesn't have it, Dinah is halfway across the country, and the fat doctor and his wife haven't spoken to the root of the clan for years."

"What about your mother?"

"I just hit her for the money I lost in the game. I couldn't go *right* back."

"I thought you did just that when you found her body."

Lukas' two glasses were empty again and he signaled for another round. "That was the plan I had," he said. "I figured if I took out the loan, I could pay it back in four or five weeks, because by then I could return to my mother and get some more cash."

"Rather indulgent, wasn't she?" Marty asked.

"Indulgent? I had to fight for every damn penny. But I always got it. She never could refuse me anything if I worked on her hard enough."

"And still she threw you out," Bill Finney murmured.

The look Lukas gave him was far from friendly.

Marty, in his turn, regarded Lukas Fenimore distastefully. *A shame to waste money on the rich.*

"What are you staring at?" Lukas abruptly demanded.

"Nothing much."

"You care to explain that?"

"It disgusts me the way some people throw away money."

"Listen to me, pill stuffer, money is *shit*. What do you think about *that?*"

"It's damned easy to talk when you've had it handed to you all your life."

Lukas laughed, a harsh, contemptuous sound. "Why should I work when I don't have to? My mother tossed me out on my ass, okay, that was her privilege, but I made sure she didn't forget it. I want every penny that's coming to me for that action."

## My Son, the Druggist

Marty shook his head disgustedly as he glanced at his roommate. "Rich in name only," he remarked.

Lukas poked Bill Finney. "Look," he crowed, "I offend the middle-class pill packer because I spit on his Great Green God. Hey, creep," he addressed Marty, "take a look at this." He took a dollar bill from his wallet, tossed it in an ashtray and fired it with a match. It curled and writhed in the flame and died in carbon. "What do you think of your almighty buck now, huh?" Lukas sneered, trying unsuccessfully to focus upon the pharmacist.

"I'll tell you what I think," Marty said quietly. "You make me sick, you and your sad ego. Instead of destroying that buck, you could've bought a kid a toy with it, or mailed it to the Cancer fund. Or given it to a hungry bum. But those things wouldn't have been nearly as dramatic as setting it on fire, would they?"

Lukas said nothing.

Marty turned to his roommate. "I've had enough of him. Ready to go?" Bill Finney shook his head. "Well, you're welcome to stay," said Marty, rising.

Lukas tried to think of something to say to Marty, but failed. He stared at him as he walked out.

Since Monday was his day off, Marty tried to salvage the remainder of it at the library. He stopped home for his Elmer Snowden folder, and while he was there, called Loretta Hamilton. There was no answer, so he tried Carol Blum.

"Well," she greeted him, "I'm surprised to hear from you, after the way you acted."

He gritted his teeth at her Oxford Circle twang.

"The way *I* acted?" he echoed.

"I was *very* embarrassed in front of my aunt. You could've talked to me, said 'drop dead' at least."

He was tempted, but let the opportunity pass.

"And how about the way you behaved at The Sleave Joint?" he demanded.

"The way *I* behaved? You were the one who ran out on me!"

Marty didn't believe what he was hearing. He was unable to find words to deal with her colossal *chutzpah*.

"Are you still there?" she asked.

"Yeah."

"Look, don't call me again. I don't know what kind of trouble you're mixed up in, but don't put *me* in the middle."

"What are you talking about?"

"I'm talking about the policeman who called about you."

*Oy, already?*

"What did you tell him?"

"He asked me about Thanksgiving night, and I told him the truth."

*For a change, Carol?*

"What exactly did you tell him?"

"I said you took me for a walk, then ran out on me."

Marty stared at the phone as if it contained a serpent. He could still hear her voice filtering through as he hung up, not gently.

He immediately phoned the police, but Chubb was out.

He briefly considered calling his partner, Dick Napoleon, to tell him about the forthcoming capital, but the thought made him feel too much like Lukas, so he put it aside for the time being.

Another meeting with the policeman was inevitable, Marty realized. He tried to get it out of his mind by thinking about Melinda.

*She actually digs me!*

The voice of Marty's mental Herbie had something to say on the subject. "You've got your tenses wrong, bubbaleh. 'She dug you.' Way back when."

*Dig, dug, so what? I didn't think she even knew I existed.*

"What difference does it make, Martillah? She's married."

*Happily?*

"Not the point. You wouldn't become involved, anyway."

*Wouldn't I?*

"A shicksah . . ."

*But she likes me!*

"Liked."

*Likes. I went after her crummy brother for her.*

"But, Marty, a shicksah . . ."

Which reminded him of Loretta Hamilton, which reminded him of Inspector Chubb.

At the library, he finally found what he was after. After searching fruitlessly through volume after volume of *Motion Picture Annual*, he located an entry in the 1931–32 edition which read . . .

SMASH YOUR BAGGAGE, Warner Brothers, Elmer Snowden and His Small's Paradise Orchestra. Ten-minute featurette in WB's musical short series. Popular Harlem swing band portrays Pullman porters in railroad station holding 4 a.m. rehearsal for their Brotherhood meeting. Selections: "Bugle Call Rag," "Tiger Rag," "Stop the Sun, Stop the Moon," "Concentratin' on You." *One reel.*

He finally knew the year and the production company! If it was Warner Brothers, that meant that in 1931 or '32, it may have been filmed out in Brooklyn, probably after Snowden's group finished the evening show. One of his film-collector friends could probably track it down and—

Marty looked up, puzzled. He had the sixth-sense sensation of being watched. He swung around to study the other browsers in the reading room, but he detected no furtive movements, no newspapers suddenly raised.

He thought about the policeman again, then about Carol. *Why the hell did she kiss me, anyway?*

Herb Adelstein had called it a taunt, an "eat-your-heart-out-sucker" kiss, just to show Marty what—

*There, I saw him!*

It was the slightest of telltales, but this time when Marty pivoted in his seat, he noticed a young man a few tables away staring at him. It was only for a fraction of a second, and the other looked down at the book before him.

*Oh, hell, it doesn't have to mean anything. Maybe he's gay.*

Marty folded up his papers, rose and put away the books he'd borrowed. He stuck the Snowden file under his arm and walked to the elevators.

The young man rose.

The elevator arrived before the other was near enough to ride in it, and Marty relaxed. But when he got off at the first floor, the other was already there, studiously scrutinizing a bulletin board.

Marty hurried to a public telephone and dialed Loretta Hamilton's number. She picked it up on the third ring.

"Loretta, this is Marty Gold. I—"

She hung up.

He thought over the alternatives, decided to grab a cab and see her. He was already connected with her in Chubb's mind, so what difference did it make?

During the ride, he kept looking behind to see if he was still being followed, but it was impossible to be sure.

When the cab pulled up in front of the Riverside Drive apartment, Cholly Gallagher was on the curb, sweeping. He saw Marty, stepped over and opened the door for him.

"Yo, Mart, I was just thinkin' about you."

"Look, Cholly, I have to take care of something important."

"There was this cop, see, asking about you."

"Yeah, I know."

"It's about old lady Fenimore, right?"

"Right." Marty tried to shove past the doorman, but Cholly planted himself in his path.

"Hey, look, Mart, I hope I didn't get ya in any trouble, but I really didn't see ya come out the other day."

"I know, Cholly, I know."

Marty brushed past and put his hand on the front-door handle. Cholly stayed right behind him.

"Y'ask me, Mart, they oughtta find that character who kept coming to see her the last couple weeks."

Marty hesitated. "What character? Coming to see who? Mrs. Fenimore?"

"Yeah, some rocky guy in a trench coat, looked like he was in the mobs."

Marty tried to picture her relatives, but neither Lukas, Rush, nor McKaye seemed to fit the description. He asked Cholly whether he knew the Fenimore clan by sight.

"I know that fruit Luke, and the daughter with the cute behind. This guy never came with them."

"Was he here recently?"

"Day before she got it."

"Did you tell the police?"

"Uh-huh. They said they were gonna send around one of those artsy-fartsy guys, y'know? Kind that draws up pictures. But they haven't yet."

Marty shrugged. "I guess they know what they're doing. I'm going up to the Hamilton pad. Don't bother to ring."

Cholly's eyes narrowed. "*Loretta* Hamilton, the blonde?"

"Uh-huh."

"Jeez, you makin' *that?*"

*Shlub's got one thing on the mind only.*

Gallagher refused to let him go up without buzzing, which saved Marty the trip because she refused to allow him in. The doorman hung up the phone and shrugged.

"She ain't too happy, I guess, since I let the other cop up before, Mart."

"I guess not."

Cholly punched him lightly on the arm, a friendly gesture. "Don't let it worry ya. She sleeps all around, you don't want her."

Marty looked curiously at him. It was the first time Gallagher had ever treated him with any kind of sympathy. *I must be in a worse mess than I realize. I actually appreciate it.*

He took a long time walking home, sorting out his thoughts. One batch concerned his relationships—or the lack of them—with Loretta Hamilton, Carol Blum and Melinda Fenimore, though not in that order. The other mental tangle involved the dead woman.

*If she didn't take those tablets deliberately, how did they get inside her body? It's pretty hard to force-feed someone medicine.*

But could it have been done? He considered the idea, only to reject it.

*When she phoned, she was already feeling sick, but she didn't know why. That eliminates the idea of somebody shoving the stuff down her throat.*

Which meant the substance had to be introduced much more subtly, insidiously. How? In food in her refrigerator? Maybe in the wine she occasionally drank? In that case, though, the killer would have had to return to destroy—

*The killer?*

The upsetting phrase brought him to an abrupt halt. Up to that time, he was chiefly concerned with the victim. He hadn't really seriously given thought to the existence of a killer, even though Chubb had indicated there might be one.

There was no time to consider it further. He was at his front door. He let himself in with his key, pushed the elevator button, then noticed the "Out of Order" sign the super had fabricated out of a torn piece of shirt cardboard.

*Again it doesn't work, again?*

He climbed the four flights laboriously, stopping at every half-floor to catch his breath. The climb would have been easier if he could have supported himself on the railing, but it was too filthy to touch.

When he reached his apartment, puffing and panting, he was surprised to find his roommate still dressed, sitting on the dilapidated green armchair.

Marty nodded wearily and dropped the Snowden folder on his desk. "Did you stay with that shmuck Lukas long?" he asked.

"Marty," Bill Finney murmured, gesturing with a slight jerk of his head, "you have company."

Marty turned and saw his mother perched uncomfortably on a wooden kitchen chair. She still had her coat buttoned to the chin—though if either of her sons had waited indoors in such a condition, she would have set their ears buzzing. Her legs were tucked up to keep her feet from touching a floor which she was sure doubled as a playing field for roachly soccer matches.

"Martin," she said seriously, "I want you to tell me what kind of trouble you're in."

Marty glanced at his roommate, but Finney shrugged.

"Not guilty, Herr Gold. Your mother was waiting outside when I arrived. I merely let her in. She refused to take off her coat." The actor glanced at the woman and raised his eyebrows quizzically. "Mrs. Gold, would you prefer speaking with your son alone?"

"Absolutely not!" she said positively. "Ida Gold don't chase no one out of their own home!"

Marty pulled over another kitchen chair and sat facing his mother. "Okay, Ma," he said, "what gives?"

She shook her head in a manner she reserved for news of premature fatalities and aggression against Israel. "To think," she moaned, "to think my son would be mixed up with the police. I didn't raise him to be a *mentsch?* Then where did I go wrong?"

"Damn it!" Marty swore. "They came and bothered you, too, Mom?"

"Oh, so you know about it? I'm glad you don't try to deny—"

"Stop talking like I'm guilty! I didn't do anything!"

She nodded her head dolefully. "Would you mind perhaps informing me what it is you're not supposed to be guilty of?"

Marty and Bill exchanged glances. Neither answered the question until Ida Gold repeated it more insistently.

It was Bill Finney who brought himself to say the word.

Marty didn't know what to expect from her. Would she turn white? Faint? Start to cry, perhaps?

She did none of those things.

"What kind of nonsense is this?" she snapped, eyes narrowed, lips quivering in anger. "Is that policeman altogether *meshuginah*? Where does he get off thinking you would do such a thing? Maybe he thinks you go around mugging people for nickels and dimes?" She rose and stormed over to the telephone.

"Ma, what are you doing?"

"Calling the police! Whatever his name is, I'll find out where he is, and believe me, will I give *him* an earful!"

He stepped swiftly to the phone and depressed the receiver. "Ma! Sit!"

She did.

"All right," said Marty, "these are the facts: one of my customers died of a drug reaction. It's unlikely she deliberately took the stuff herself, so the fuzz—"

"Speak English," she admonished.

Marty stared at the ceiling for a second, then patiently continued. "The police are trying to find out how it happened, and there's reason to think she might have deliberately been—"

"Who is *she*? Doesn't she have a name?" his mother demanded.

"Her last name was Fenimore."

His mother's eyes widened. "Not Bernice Fenimore?"

"You knew her?"

"Did she live on Riverside Drive? Over near the marina?"

"That's her," Marty said, surprised. "I had no idea you and she had ever met."

"Years ago, Marty, years ago. Once she was active at Beth Jeshuron, but that was before you were born."

*I'm hearing things.* Marty blinked, asked his mother to repeat what she'd said.

"But she wasn't Jewish," he protested.

"Yes and no," said Ida Gold. "She married a goy." She made a forestalling gesture toward Bill Finney. "You should pardon the expression."

"I *have* heard the word, Mrs. Gold."

"I'm sure," she acknowledged. "Anyhow, there was a big tsimmis with her husband over her being so active at temple, and then to top things off, the rabbi—the old one, Rabbi Gershon, you didn't know him, Martillah—"

"Never *mind*, Ma!" Marty interjected, fearing the interminable historic details would never stop.

"Anyhow, to make a long story short, she gave up her religion, or so we were supposed to think. *I* know she was just trying to please her husband. But there's a limit. She should have put her foot down with the children, but the boy never got Bar Mitzvah'd and two of the girls, I hear, married *goyim*, and it must've broken Bernice's heart. That's what *I* think!" Without any transition at all, she returned to the problem of her son and the police. "What makes them think you, of all people, would hurt that poor old lady? What reason could you possibly have?"

Marty mentioned the ten-thousand-dollar bequest.

His mother shook her head in disbelief. "That policeman has kishkas for brains! For ten thousand dollars, who can live even a year in this city? What kind of goon would go to such trouble for such a furshtunkinah amount?"

Marty laughed in spite of himself. Then a thought occurred to him, and his mirth died. "Mom," he asked worriedly, "what does Dad have to say about all this?"

"Your father? Thank God he was not at home when the officer called! He was fixing Mabel Asthalter's TV, on a house call, so he doesn't know from a thing, and if I can help it, that's the way it'll stay. His shenanigans I'm in no mood to tolerate, especially if he were to hear what this mess is all about. He'll punch that cop in the nose and that'll be the end of it, I'll have to sell my ring to meet his bail!"

Mrs. Gold started to get up.

"You'll excuse me, I'd better get home before he arrives, he's got to go out tonight to a lodge meeting." She sighed profoundly. "Marty, you know he's not allowed to ask you to join. Why don't you talk to him already, it'd make him so happy?"

"Ma, I don't want to join the Masons!"

"No, you'd rather run around with that other crazy bunch of idiots. God knows what you do there."

"The Sons of the Desert," Marty patiently explained, "is a film society."

"To me, they sound like Arabs."

He raised his hands in exasperation. "Forget it, okay? Before you go, tell me what the policeman asked you."

"He wanted to know about Thanksgiving night, and I had to give him Carol's phone number. So I figured, 'Gevalt, Marty took her to some kind of pot party!'"

"How many times do I have to tell you, I'm not into that kind of thing?" As he spoke, he took her to the elevator. It still wasn't working.

"This," said Mrs. Gold, starting down the stairs, "is another thing I won't tell your father about. You know him! He'd only want to know why you want to live like an animal when you have a nice home to come back to. I never know what to answer him when he starts on that . . ."

Her words trailed off as she descended the stairs and passed from view. Marty wondered if she'd stopped talking, or if she was just out of earshot.

Back in the apartment, Bill Finney had changed to underwear and bathrobe. *Now he looks more natural.* The actor suggested making drinks, but Marty held up a hand to prevent a minor libationary disaster.

"I'll fix something this time, Bill."

Once they had scotches-and-water in their hands, they sat down opposite each other. Bill Finney took a long sip, then spoke.

"You may not believe it, but you made a slight dent in friend Lukas' armor. A *slight* one."

"I'm thrilled," said Marty.

"I'm sorry I had to tell the inspector about your interlude with Ms. Hamilton, but I felt it best that you level with him."

"Mm-hm," Marty murmured, "only I didn't. And as far as she's concerned, I might as well forget about any further interludes."

"One thing at a time," the actor said. "What do you mean, you didn't level with him?"

Marty explained about Carol Blum's Thanksgiving evening jaunt, and how he'd pretended that he'd had her out all night.

"And now she herself has blown the whistle on you? A charming wench."

"Her I can do without. But I'm sorry they went and questioned Loretta."

"She could only corroborate that you were there. It was fortunate they did have her name. At least one of your stories will check out. And as far as her favors are concerned, *mein freund,* it strikes me you are not liberated enough to support such a situation *in extensio.*"

Marty sighed. "I expect you're right."

*Come off it, you're not even thinking of Loretta.*

He swallowed the rest of his scotch, refilled it and swirled the liquid gently against the ice.

His roommate watched him.

"You're nervous, Apothecary," he proclaimed.

"Brilliant, my florid physician! How can you tell?"

"I shouldn't despair just yet. Perhaps the inspector will merely reprimand you."

"Yeah? When *would* you start to worry? When he begins to read off my rights?"

The telephone rang. Bill Finney was closer to the instrument than Marty, but it was too difficult a feat of engineering for him to get up, so Marty rose and answered it.

"Come over to the store," Herb Adelstein said.

"Now? On my day off?"

"Lou asked me to call."

"But it's almost time to close."

"Uh-huh. Lou wants to talk to you in private. Says it's urgent."

Marty hung up. He stared at the phone in baffled concern, then reached for his still-damp snowshoes and started to pull them back on.

His roommate said nothing.

*One of the great things about him is he knows when to keep his trap shut.*

Bill Finney went silently to the kitchen with Marty's glass, poured in another half ounce of scotch and proffered it.

Marty gratefully accepted.

Spector hurried the last customer out, insisted that Herbie leave too, locked the door and returned to the prescription counter. He and Marty were alone in the store.

Spector had on an old gray sweater and his pinstripe blue suit pants, and he looked cold. Marty watched him rubbing his five-o'clock growth of whiskers with the palm of one hand. He was evidently reluctant to begin. His fingers pinched the end of his scraggly mustache and tugged in a preoccupied manner. At last, he cleared his throat.

"Marty," he said, "the cop came around asking more questions."

"I figured he would."

"He was mostly asking about you."

Marty nodded. "That's no surprise."

"He shows up just when I'm ass-over-elbows occupied trying to get another rush to the Home. He says, 'Go ahead, if it's urgent, I'll just wait,' only he makes me nervous standing at my side and I'm afraid I'll mess something up, so I say, 'Damn it, ask what you want and do it now, and hurry it up!' So he does."

"What all did he want to know about me?"

"Everything. When I hired you, and why. If you ever give me trouble. How you get along with customers, especially old ladies like Fenimore."

"Christ!" Marty swore. "He think I'm trying to get in every *alte cocker's* will?"

"The part that worries me most," said Spector, "is the

questions he asked about how you make up prescriptions."

"The procedure?"

"Yeah, but more than that. Not just the general details, he wanted to find out my exact recollection of where you were standing when you filled her Darvon prescription, whether you followed the usual routine, or if I saw you do anything unusual. Like I have time to watch you every minute, or something."

"Why would he ask all that?" Marty asked, then immediately waved his hand in a deprecating gesture. "Never mind, that's a stupid question, I already know why."

Spector nodded. "So you see, anyhow, why I had to talk to you today."

Marty sat on a fountain stool and rested his elbows on the marble counter. It felt pleasantly cool through the fabric of his shirtsleeves.

"Jesus, Mary and Joseph," he murmured, immediately and irrelevantly reflecting on the lack of satisfying swear words in the Anglo-Jewish vernacular. *"Abraham, Isaac and Jacob" just doesn't make it . . .*

He snapped his fingers. "Maybe Herbie saw me."

"Uh-uh. He was getting a tooth yanked, remember?"

"Oh. Yeah." Marty was starting to get a headache.

Spector took off his lab coat and draped it carefully over a hanger (lest his wife complain), then hung it in the closet. He walked over to his assistant and put a hand gently on his back.

"Marty, I hate to say this."

"Say what? Don't tell me you're starting to think I'm capable—"

"Naah, naah, I know you'd never deliberately hurt anybody, only . . ."

"Only *what?*" Marty asked, raising his voice.

Spector shrugged. "You might've made an honest mistake."

"An *honest* mistake?" Marty echoed. "What kind of honest mistake is it that kills someone? If I could do that, maybe I shouldn't have a license! Maybe—"

"Marty, shecket!" Spector called for silence in Hebrew. "Now, look, there are lots of mistakes that go on in this business. We carry here, what, maybe twenty-seven thousand different drugs out of a hundred thousand available on the market, and—"

"Lou, for God's sake!" Marty jumped up from the stool. "We're not talking about minor mistakes. Anybody can misread a prescription and give somebody Librium instead of Librax. The words are similar, the pills are similar, even the insides are similar. And sure, sometimes I don't always have time to call Doc Paul and get him to decipher his handwriting, whether he means quinine or quinity, or I figure he wants Ornade and it's really Ornase. It happens to every druggist, and nothing awful happens. But you're talking about the difference between Darvon and Butazolidin Alka—capsules shaped differently and colored distinctly. Lou, if I was such a total *shlemiel* to take down the Butazolidin supply instead of the Darvon container, I'd turn in my license!"

"Will you let me finish?" Spector asked. "There's another kind of accident that could've happened."

"What?"

"Where were you when you made up her prescription?"

"Right behind the counter."

"Where was I?"

"Same place. On my left."

"Uh-huh." Spector nodded slowly. Then he beckoned Marty to look at one of the drug-record books which lay open to a certain page.

After a moment, Marty raised his head and stared quizzically at his boss.

"You really think I could've done that?"

Spector shook his head slowly. "But it's possible, isn't it?"

"It's possible. But it didn't happen."

A long silence.

"The question is," said Spector at last, "whether to hold on to it, or give it to the cop before he calls again?"

Marty felt too miserable to reply.

Tuesday was a nightmare of mindless routine and irrelevant questions. The business of the store ground on, and Etta Spector complained about the expenses, which she was still unnecessarily engaged in double-checking against the computer service that handled the Spector's Drugs account.

"Louie, what do we need with all these magazines?" she shouted. "They all say the same thing." She was referring to the numerous pharmaceutical trade publications her husband subscribed to.

"I need 'em to keep up," he growled.

"Since when have you got time to read?"

"They're deductible. Now leave me alone with the goddamn magazines!"

His more than usually agitated response cowed his wife for all of thirty seconds—and then she was off on another budgetary harangue.

Marty and Spector hardly looked at each other, nor did they speak.

Meanwhile, Herb Adelstein was busy with the non-pharmaceutical stock and had his own sour mood to contend with.

"Lou, I've gotta throw some of this junk out, there's not enough space for holiday merchandise."

"Throw out?" Spector bellowed. "Who's gonna pay for it? You?"

"I only have so much room! Where should I put the specials?"

"Louie!" his wife warned, "don't say it!"

"Make a pile," said Spector. "I'll see what can go and what can't."

Spector lumbered over to the housewares-cosmetics aisle and began to inspect the goods his employee wished to discard. He picked up a heavy glass bottle full of green liquid. "Right away," he said, "this stays! You know how much it cost me?"

"But Lou," the other protested, "who the hell is going to buy a fifty-buck bottle of perfume?"

"Some drunk, December twenty-fourth, two minutes before closing, will come in and want something, and the rest of the stock'll be all sold out . . ."

"Okay," Herb sighed, "but let me put some of this other *dreck* in a dump bin and sell the whole batch at a discount."

"Do what you want," Spector said, no longer interested. He walked slowly back to the prescription counter, shaking his head, murmuring to himself.

Just as Etta Spector was beginning to put on her coat to go home and make dinner for her husband, the door opened and Inspector Abner Chubb walked in. He had a grim, purposeful air about him, and when she saw the policeman, the Old Lady immediately removed her coat and hung it up again.

Loretta Hamilton was the only customer in the store. Marty offered to wait on her, but she passed him by for Herb Adelstein. The latter glanced quizzically at Gold but said nothing.

When she was gone, Chubb beckoned Marty to approach, and he did. The policeman spoke, wasting no time on polite formalities.

"You lied. What were you doing Thanksgiving evening after you left Carol Blum?"

"I went straight home."

"Why didn't you tell me that the first time?"

Out of the corner of his eye, Marty saw Spector and Herbie whispering to one another. With difficulty, he swallowed and told Chubb the tale of his misguided attempt to cover Carol's indiscretion.

"Anyone see you go home?"

"No. My roommate was asleep when I arrived."

"All right. You'd better get your things."

Chubb was expecting an argument, but the druggist walked to the closet without comment, removed his lab jacket and began to don topcoat and galoshes.

"Before you take him anywhere," Spector said to Chubb, "I want to talk to you."

Marty objected. "Lou, I'll tell him later."

"Naah. Now." He nodded to Herb Adelstein, who went to the front door and locked it, flipping the "Closed" sign.

Chubb watched with perplexity and mistrust.

Spector gestured toward the stock with a broad flip of his large hand. "Y'see that? Twenty-seven thousand drugs, a good two hundred of which are on regular call. To top—"

The phone rang. Spector grabbed it, dealt with the customer as quickly as possible, hung up and resumed.

"Between the federal and state forms and records we have to fill out and keep, you can go buggy. You get the medicine in ten seconds, maybe, count out the dosage spec in maybe a minute—and then fill forms and type labels for a goddamn half hour! The same rigmarole routine, even if you've got a prescription for a placebo."

Chubb looked impatient, but Spector ignored the policeman's evident desire for him to be done. "What I'm saying is how easy it is to make a mistake. We all goof. Marty, here, may have done something unintentional when he was filling the Darvon prescription for Mrs. Fenimore."

Spector held up the pill-counting tray. "We use this gizmo to keep from handling the medicine with our fingers. The pills are spilled out of the big container onto the surface and we prod the correct number into the customer's bottle with a spatula or knife or tongue depressor. Then we type up a label and stick it on the outside of the vial."

"So?" Chubb asked, bored.

"*So*, I remember when Marty was making up the Darvon refill for Fenimore, the phone rang and it was for him, he had to go talk to his mother before he could do the label. Meantime, I've checked the books, and that morning I made up a prescription for Butazolidin."

Chubb said nothing.

Marty continued it. "What Lou thinks is I stuck the label on Lou's bottle by accident, gave her the wrong medicine and she swallowed it without looking, thinking the pills were Darvon."

The policeman shook his head. "Then, where'd the Darvon come from in her cabinet? It had the right label."

Marty turned to his employer. "I *told* you. And if there'd been a mix-up, wouldn't we have heard from the other customer?"

Chubb said, "I think there *was* a mix-up, but not like the one you've described."

"Meaning?" Spector asked.

"When we found her body, the Darvon bottle was standing in the kitchen, on the countertop, and there was an unrinsed glass in the sink."

"So?"

"Did you see her place? Spotless. Nothing out of place. Five'll get you ten she washed glasses practically as fast as she used them, put away everything in its proper place."

Marty nodded. "Sounds like her. You're saying, then, the attack must've happened shortly after she took her Darvon that morning?"

"I'm saying that, ruling out suicide, she had to ingest the Butazolidin somehow. Nobody stuck it down her throat. She mostly ate alone. But she was suffering from bursitis pain, and was taking Darvon regularly. She might well have taken a couple of doctored Darvons with the other drug stuffed inside. Could it be done?"

Spector nodded reluctantly.

There was a brief, uncomfortable silence. Marty spoke.

"Have you checked the Darvons remaining?"

The policeman nodded. "We took samples from each. It's all Darvon."

"So you have no evidence, really," said Spector. "Just a surmisal."

Chubb spread his hands in a gesture which told them nothing of what he might or might not be thinking.

But Marty was sure he understood.

"What you're suggesting is that I stuffed some Butazolidin in one or two of her Darvon capsules, and then stuck them on top of her regular Darvon prescription."

"I'm not suggesting anything," Chubb said dourly. "Get your coat."

"*When?*" an unexpected voice shrilled.

Everyone's head turned.

The officer looked puzzled. Three parallel furrows creased his forehead. "What do you mean, 'when'?"

"*When!* When is *when,* Mister Big-Shot Cop!" Etta Spector expressed herself with immense scorn. "When do you think my boytchick"—She gestured toward Marty—"would have the chance to do such a thing as you're 'not suggesting'? *Hah?*"

"Look, Mrs. Spector," Abner Chubb began politely, "what difference does it make when he did it? *If* he did it," he added hastily. "It could be while he was making up the prescription, or it could have been prepared beforehand and—"

"*Hah?*" the Old Lady turned to Herb Adelstein. "Is he talking, or ain't I hearing, *hah?*"

"Etta, shah," Spector murmured.

"You *shah!*" she told her husband sternly. "What kind of man are you, Louie, that even for a minute you would believe a decent boy like our Martillah would do this, even by accident?"

Marty blinked in amazement.

*She's defending me? The Old Lady?*

She waggled a finger at the inspector. "Listen good, *balagool!* First off, this is impossible for Marty to empty out one kind of medicine capsule and shovel the powder into the empties of another kind—all with my Louie working right next to him! And such a thing don't take ten seconds to do, anyway, or maybe you think we go one-two-three, it's a pill? *Hah?*"

Chubb wanted to speak, but she impatiently gestured for silence. "Don't give me from your other song and dance, I've got brains, I can figure! This leaves, what I say, just one possibility. That Marty would make up such a pill beforehand and wait and wait until Bernice should have another attack of her bursitis, and run out of her old Darvons. This, itself, is ridiculous! But say he did. Then he'd have to sneak the pill into the middle of the real ones while he was counting them and be careful to make sure it got in to the medicine bottle." She pointed to the Darvon pulvules her husband had counted; they were still resting on the counting tray. "Take a look. Could *you* tell one from the other?"

"There would be no need to," Chubb argued, "as long as the prepared capsule got anywhere into the—"

"Dummy!" she interrupted. "The prescription calls for maybe twenty pills, he spills out, who knows, maybe twenty-three, so if he's counting, he's got to keep an eye— a very careful eye—on the one or two funny pills. This he don't do!"

"How do *you* know he didn't?" Chubb asked, unconvinced.

"Because I watched him make up the prescription! He was so busy talking to Bernice, he didn't pay attention to what he was doing. Three times he loses count, he's got to spill all the pills back in the middle of the tray and start over. By that time, they're all good and mixed up. And, when he finally gets them all inside, he fishes one out for her to swallow so she shouldn't have to put up with the pain a second longer than necessary. Would he do that if he wanted to kill her? Risk her having the attack even before she leaves the store, *hah?*"

Marty slapped his hand against his forehead. "I forgot I gave her a pill!"

"Nu? So you, too, are a dummy," the Old Lady proclaimed.

"The pill could've been the first to go in the bottle, then he could've just left it there while he was counting the others again," Chubb said.

"So smart you are!" the Old Lady sneered. "Maybe it jumped off the bottom and into her mouth? Or do you think she takes pills upside down?" Her lips curled in a disgusted moue.

Chubb wrote rapidly in his notebook. After a few minutes, during which Marty scarcely breathed, the policeman pointed his pencil at Etta Spector.

"So you're trying to tell me that of all the hundreds of thousands of prescriptions you must've seen Mr. Gold write, you actually remember this *one* in detail?"

"You're trying to tell *me* something happens in this store I don't know about?" she squawked. "All right, listen, Hot-Shot, that morning I'm waiting for Marty to stop yapping with Bernice Fenimore so he can take over the register for me. My Louie is busy, this other clown is out with a bad tooth, the stock boy I wouldn't let within ten feet of the money, so I'm waiting for Marty and I'm watching every move he's making till he'll finally get finished before I make pish on the floor!"

Herb Adelstein guffawed, then stifled it as she shot him a nasty glance. Chubb shuffled from one foot to the other, momentarily embarrassed.

*Trouble with being so bald. You turn red too easy.*

"Nu?" she demanded, arms akimbo. "Are you done now, or do you got more trouble to make my Marty?"

*"My Marty?" Vey's mir, tomorrow she'll make me dust the ceiling!*

## My Son, the Druggist

"I'm not done," Chubb retorted. "Mr. Gold started his own troubles, *not* me. First he withheld information about the time he spent with Mrs. Hamilton, then he lied—"

"Marty don't lie!" she said with conviction. Then the words caught up with her. *"Mrs. Hamilton?"*

Turning slowly, she fixed Marty with an icy stare. *Gevalt, why didn't I just let him arrest me?*

"—and second," Chubb continued, "there's the problem of several unaccounted hours on Thanksgiving. Which is important because there's still the possibility of the Darvon being fixed after Mrs. Fenimore brought them home. The most likely time someone could've had access to them was Thanksgiving day or evening. I questioned the doormen. The only way in without a key is through the front door. There was only one occasion when someone might've gotten past without being seen. Unfortunately, Mr. Gold lied about being tied up all night at his parents', and it's not inconceivable that he slipped in while the entryway was clear—"

"Slow down, slow down," said Spector. "What kind of business is this? Either the doorman's there, or the front door is locked, right?"

Chubb shook his head. "He could've rung Mrs. Fenimore and had her buzz him through, then exited later through the basement. The cellar doors work one way without a key. You can get out but not in."

"So where was the doorman?"

"Chasing a kid up the street. Some brat came in and caused trouble."

Marty interrupted. "Cholly Gallagher?"

"Uh-huh."

"Does he remember what time that was?"

"Eight-thirty."

*The crud!*

"At eight-thirty," Marty said precisely, "I was *still* having dinner with my parents. As I think I mentioned to you."

*Only remembers the damaging details. Maybe he doesn't like my last name.*

Chubb hastily thumbed through his notebook. He found the information he sought, looked up sheepishly and admitted he'd overlooked the salient fact.

Herbie moved forward to pat Marty on the back, and as he did, Marty heard him mumble something about suing the police department for character defamation.

Chubb must have caught it, too, because he said a great many apologetic things as he veered toward the magnetic pole of the front door. When he was gone, Spector heartily shook his employee's hand, and Herb slapped his back again.

"You fake!" he told Marty. "You were shtupping Hamilton all the time!"

Marty winced. He knew Etta Spector was still riveting him with a frigid glare.

"Chubby Abe in?" the chunky lieutenant asked.

"Yeah, but don't bug 'im, G.R. He's in a cruddy mood."

"Got to. Murder one."

"Then *you* tell 'im," the desk sergeant declared, jerking a thumb at the closed door.

He knocked, and Chubb told him to enter. The inspector waved him to a seat.

"Just going to call you, George. What's up?"

"Private, name of Jack Cohen, got his brains blasted in his office. Eighty-third and West End."

"Anything snatched?"

The lieutenant spread his hands, palms up. "Want me to get on over?"

"I'll take it," said Chubb. "I've got a warrant for you to get grinding."

"On Fenimore?"

"Mm-hm. Tough. But I'm playing probabilities."

Chubb told the detective his assignment. The lieutenant nodded and left.

Sighing, the inspector unwrapped a stale sandwich and munched it. Between bites, he rang up the desk sergeant and ordered the sedan.

It was going to be a long night.

After the roaring lion, the blipping radio tower, the deep gong stroke and the drone of the early 1930s airplane, a succession of fanfares shook the walls of the apartment. Then a band struck up a lively tune, and Abbott and Costello sang:

> Laugh, laugh, laugh,
> There's lots to be thankful for!
> Laugh, laugh, laugh,
> Things have been worse before!

Bill Finney snapped off the tape recorder. "It sounds fine," he said unenthusiastically.

Marty nodded, referring to a sheet of paper. "They're all there. In order: MGM, RKO, J. Arthur Rank, early Universal, Warner Brothers, Paramount and Vistavision, MCA, nineteen-forties Universal, Twentieth-Century Fox. All the Abbott and Costello discs they made, KKK label stuff, Willie Howard, Chaplin, Noah Beery singing 'The Whip,' Conrad Veidt—he'll flip when he hears *that* one—"

The tape was a long-promised project for Bill Finney's brother in Oregon. Marty had been compiling it a bit at a time, and picked that evening to play his roommate the first side.

"He's been expecting it *so* long," Marty explained, "I thought it'd be appropriate to start with all the old movie openings and fanfares."

Bill Finney glanced uncomfortably at Herb Adelstein in the other chair. Herb shrugged, bored.

"Herr Gold," the huge actor grumbled, "I appreciate the effort, but it can wait."

Marty switched the tape on, sped it forward. "Just let me play you the Klan stuff—by the '100% Americans.'" He glanced over at Herb. "You won't know how to react. It's funny and horrible at the same time."

"Martillah," Herb groaned, "you played it for me before."

"I did?"

Herb nodded. "All of them: 'Mystic City,' 'Daddy Stole My Last Clean Sheet—'"

"'—to join the Ku Klux Klan,'" Bill Finney finished the title.

"Well, did I ever play you any of the Horrible Label songs? They're—"

"Deliberately horrible." Herb nodded. "We've heard 'em!"

Marty gestured impatiently. "Okay, what *do* you want to hear? Rag? Dixieland? 'The Cross of Gold?' You tell me."

"Nothing!"

"What else, then? A round of knucks?"

Waving a hand in dismissal of the suggestion, Herb ambled over to the refrigerator and took out a bottle of Beck's. He plucked the magnetic church key off the side of the machine and prized away the cap. "Christ," he grunted, "you're manic tonight." His thin neck straightened as he poured the beer down his throat.

"What the hell you expect, a funeral?" Marty asked. "Maybe you came over to hand-hold the reprieved pariah?"

"What *I* came for," Herb said between swallows, "is to hear all about that cute blond tush."

"Forget it," Marty replied. He stared grimly at his hands. "Anything happened for the last week, I'm not discussing."

The downstairs doorbell rang.

"You expecting somebody?" Marty asked. His roommate shook his head. "Wish to hell we had an intercom," Marty murmured, walking to the wall button and pressing it.

"Use the peephole," Herb suggested.

"Gee, I would've never thought of that," his friend remarked with heavy irony. *How long's he think I've lived in New York?*

"At least they fixed the elevator," Bill Finney observed. The whine of the ancient machine sounded through closed doors. It wheezed to a halt, and they heard the hollow reverberation of approaching footsteps, then a knock loud enough to qualify as pounding. Marty peered through the tiny safety aperture.

"Ohmigod," he breathed, "*both* of them!"

"Who?" Bill Finney demanded.

"My parents."

Both Marty's friends made a move for their coats, but he stepped in front of them.

"What am I?" he lamented. "A sinking ship?"

They couldn't find anything to say, so they sat back down. Herb grumbled, "Might as well hear it now as warmed over."

At the door, Abe Gold bellowed to be admitted and his wife's thin tones could barely be discerned ordering him to lower his voice. For reply, he banged louder with his fist.

Shaking his head, Marty looked for strength to his friends, but they had nothing to suggest, so, with a resigned shrug, he unlocked the door and swung it open.

"Ah-*hah!*" his father greeted him. "My son, the *bum.*"

Ida Gold shoved her husband aside and strode into the room. She nodded politely to Bill Finney and Herb, but barely acknowledged her son.

"I am here," she declared to all ears within hearing, "not because I want to be, but so my husband will not create such a *tsimmis* that he'll be arrested for disturbing the peace."

"I'm not disturbing no peace," her husband stated, his whiskery chins trembling indignantly. He'd been working late in the shop when Etta Spector's news had reached him via phone, and he'd come over right from his store. Under his coat he still had on his leather apron, stuffed with miscellaneous hardwares, lengths of solder and tools. "I'm here," he explained, "to have a quiet talk *alone* with the bum." He glowered expectantly at Herb Adelstein and Bill Finney, but his wife gestured for the two young men to remain seated.

"For the first thing," she said, "*I* am not budging. Second of all, my son has a guest, and it is not our house to tell who should come or go, and as for Marty's roommate, it's his house, too, and not even with such behavior as we've heard about your son will we chase out a person who belongs into the street, especially in this weather! So I'm telling you Abe—"

Abe Gold didn't wait to hear the conclusion of his wife's policy statement. "Since when," he interrupted, "is

Marty suddenly *my* son? Since when have you transferred your mortgage on him to *me*?"

"I don't know what you're talking, and lower your voice, Abe!"

"You don't know what I'm talking? In a pig's pajamas! When he was shtunking through pill school, did I want him to stop pishing away money and come learn from me, someday take over the shop? No! Then—*then*—he was *your* son! Now, he's a bum, suddenly he's mine!"

"Why am I a bum?" Marty asked ingenuously.

*Might as well lie down, the steamroller's coming anyway.*

But it was his mother who answered first. "You're a bum," she said as casually as if she were reporting on the weather, "because, instead of going out with nice girls like Carol—the way you treated *her*, don't ask!—instead of her, you fool around with tramps!"

Marty almost told his mother what Carol Blum was really like, but two things interfered. The first was a thought which suddenly occurred to him. The second was his father's bellowing.

"Not just a tramp," Abe Gold proclaimed, "but a shicksah!"

"Abraham," his wife warned.

"Look, if my son wants to room with a *shaygitz*, that's his business, provided he don't pick up no *goyishe* habits. But running around with a shicksah—"

"Abraham! You could find some other word!"

He looked at her, surprised. "Something is wrong with 'shicksah?' What would *you* call her? A *litvak*?"

"It's a lousy word!" Marty snapped.

"*Hah?*"

"The way you say it, Pop, it sounds like an insult. Like 'kike.'"

Abe Gold glared at his son. "You're calling me a kike?" His face was beet-red.

"That's *not* what I said!" Marty appealed to his mother. "I can never get through to him!"

She sniffed. "Don't talk to me, Martin, I have nothing to say to you."

Herb thought he should calm the old man down before he burst a blood vessel. "I think what Marty is trying to say, Mr. Gold, is—"

He cut him off with withering irony. "Perhaps I gave you the impression that this argument is a group discussion? Maybe you thought you heard me say, 'I should like to solicit Mr. Adelstein's opinion'?" He glanced at Bill Finney. "Maybe you, too, have something weighty to contribute?"

His wife was shocked. *"Abe!"*

"What have I done *now?*" he demanded in baffled rage.

"It is not necessary to make personal remarks."

*"What* personal remarks?"

"You practically called him fat!" she accused.

"And you would call him thin?"

Marty was livid. "I've had enough! You come into my apartment, insult my roommate—"

"Shecket!" his father roared. "This is between me and the shaygitz!" He faced Bill Finney, who was doing his best to keep a straight face. "If I said anything to hurt your feelings, I apologize," the old man said. "Okay? We square?"

The actor nodded, covering the lower part of his face with his hand.

"Something you're finding funny?"

Bill Finney shook his head, not trusting himself to speak.

"Good. If there's something ha-ha to laugh, I would like to hear it!" He confronted his son once more. "Getting back to you, bum. Not only do you fool with a shicksah, you have to pick a married one! Maybe you want to be picking lead outta your *tuchus?*"

Marty was momentarily startled, then he realized his father was still talking about Loretta Hamilton.

"Married? I thought she was divorced!"

"Dummy! Jack Hamilton is my customer, I fixed his Philco last time he was in town. He's away three, four months at a time in the merchant marine. You know what he looks like? Seven feet tall, with hands as big as my *pipick*, and he eats boilerplates for *nosh!*" He shook his head disgustedly. "*Him* you pick to mess with, dummy?"

Marty made a gesture of appeasement, pushing his hands palm-down in the air as if quieting a noisy classroom. "Look, Pop, I had no idea she wasn't divorced. From now on, believe me, I won't go within twenty feet of her, okay?" *Mainly because she won't let me.*

"All right, Abie," Marty's mother said, "you heard what you wanted to hear, let's go."

But her husband planted his feet firmly, inhaled a bucketful of air and crossed his arms expectantly. "I'm not going yet," he declared. He glowered at Marty. "That's all you're gonna tell me?"

*Now what?*

"What else do you expect?"

"From your personal lips, bummeleh, I want to hear you don't fool with no more shicksahs, period."

His wife yanked his coat. "Abe, come, this is not necessary."

"I'm not budging till he talks."

She appealed to her son with some desperation. "Marty, tell the big little man what he wants to hear, it costs you something?"

He looked at his father as he replied.

"Yeah, Ma. It costs."

On impulse, Herb Adelstein started to clap, but after a single report, immediately stuck his hands under his armpits and tried to appear nonchalant.

Abe Gold shot him a black look. "Now that my son don't live home, I see where he gets his opinions. He works with half-a-goy, lives with—" He stopped, noticing a motion in a corner of the room. He stuck a finger in that direction. "See, Ida? What did I say? He moves out, it'll be roaches and goyim!"

*"Damn it to hell, cut it out!"*

His father whirled on him. "At *me* you curse? At *me?*"

"They're my friends, not the Third Reich! They've got names, not labels!" Marty took a deep breath, exhaled, forced himself to speak more softly. "Look, Pop, my opinions, whether I've thought them all out completely, they're my *own*. I'm not going to live somebody else's idea of my life, even if it's yours."

"Sure, even if it's me," his father echoed bitterly. "The fact that I'm your father is not important, no, but also that I'm cantor of Beth Jeshuron, this, too, is of no importance? *You* could care less if the people should point at you on the *bimah* and say, 'The Chossin's son, he diddles married shicksahs on the side!'"

"Abie, please!" his wife protested.

"Listen, if that's what's eating you," Marty sighed, exhausted with the argument, "I'll make it easy. I just won't come for a while."

His father, for once, was totally unable to speak.

"To tell you the truth," Marty continued, sadly shaking his head, "I don't know where I'm at these days. Maybe the best thing I could do is just take time out, think things over . . ."

"*What* things?" his father demanded.

"The whole Jewish bit."

Abe Gold's eyes nearly bulged out of their sockets.

"A *bit?* You call it a *bit?* You think maybe you're the rabbi, *that* meshuginah?" He was referring to Rabbi Chomsky's penchant for discussing synagogue affairs in theatrical terms.

Marty looked at his mother, seeking help he knew could not be forthcoming. *I opened my yap. Stick both feet in, why don't you?*

But there was no need for further discussion. His father was already opening the door.

"Ida? You coming?"

"In a minute, Abe. I still have something I got to say to Marty."

"I have nothing else to say to *your* son," he snapped. "I'll wait downstairs."

He slammed the door so hard that the teabell rattled off the counter and fell into the sink.

Ida Gold stood by the door, waiting for the emotional atmosphere to settle before she spoke. She nodded toward

## My Son, the Druggist

Bill Finney and Herb Adelstein and briefly apologized for her husband's temper. Then she turned to Marty.

Extending a hand, she touched him gently. "Marty, later I'll spread the oil with you and your father, but right now, I want you should know, first of all, I remember you've always been a good boy. You work hard, and you don't answer back much."

*I might as well be a five-year-old.*

"Three things I want you to keep in mind while you're questioning. And listen, Marty, the first is that *everybody* questions, it's only natural!"

"Even Pop?" he asked with bitter humor.

She ignored the remark. "The second thing you should consider is a life of ritual is a beautiful thing. The answers to things in this world we don't get, and sometimes it hurts. But many, many people have believed. And if you do things a certain way, it gives—how should I put it?—a beauty, an order to what you do every day. It mounts up to a life."

Marty exchanged a meaningful glance with his roommate. He remembered an argument he'd once had with him over the value and meaning of religious tradition. "Ritual," the actor had proclaimed, "is the deliberate assignment of Purpose to purposelessness—a mystic mental pattern for avoiding the Void."

*But I can't tell her that. I don't even completely believe it myself yet.* He stubbed himself on the thought. *Yet? What do I mean by "yet?"*

Rather than consider it, he addressed his mother. "What's the third thing you want me to think about?"

"Just this, Martin: if you should ever marry a shicksah (you should pardon the word, Mr. Finney), it'll break your father's heart." She tossed her head with an air of having said all that was necessary for Marty to hear on the subject. "And now," she said, opening the door, "I'll go. Don't get up, gentlemen." (They had not made a move.) She paused, hand on knob. "I only hope you should be on speaking terms again with your father, so you can come over to the house when your brother is home on leave."

"I could meet him at the station."

"And have your father outyell the boxing meshuginahs up in Madison Square Garden? No, no, when your brother comes next week, I'll try to spread the oil. Meantime, *you* think." She stepped through the door and closed it firmly behind her.

Marty plopped into a chair. "Christ, what a night!"

"But now you are a man," Herb said. "Want a beer?"

"No."

"Listen, Martillah, I know how you feel . . . like you turned down a job when you're already out of work. But look, you actually made up your mind when you moved out."

"I don't think so."

"Sure you did."

Marty shook his head.

"All right," Herb conceded, patting his friend on the back, "so you're still looking to buy, but at least now you're reading the price tags." He cocked his head to one side in his characteristic pose, caught Bill Finney's notice and nodded toward the door. "Let's go get a beer before he asks us to get out."

"Thanks, Herb," Marty said, grateful at being anticipated.

## My Son, the Druggist

"Y'believe this guy?" Herb asked. "When we want to go, he makes us stay, but now the air raid's over, he throws us out to play in the rubble." He beckoned to the actor. "Come on, I'll treat us to boilermakers."

Bill Finney hoisted his huge butt off the chair, pulled his coat around his shoulders and bowed to his roommate. "Esteemed outcast, is there aught we can bring you back from the land of Pick and Pay?"

Marty nodded. "I *am* hungry. Get some salami. You need money?" *Dope, you even have to ask?* He tossed a pair of bills at his companion and waited for the two of them to leave before cradling his head in his hands.

*On and on. All the time, people come and go. Just like always. I argue with Pop, he yells at me. I slide off one hook, another gets stuck in my back. And all the while, before and during and after, a woman is dead. Gone. Finished.*

The telephone rang. The sudden sound made him start.

"Marty, it's me, remember?" she asked. "I thought we might talk over old times, we had so little chance and nothing was right yesterday."

His first thought was that Herb and Bill had gotten someone to play a joke on him. Then he remembered that neither knew how he felt about Melinda Fenimore. *Rush.*

"When?" he asked, automatically brushing his hand over his head to smooth the ever-present cowlick.

"Anytime. Now, if you like. I'm not busy."

He glanced at his watch. "It's after nine o'clock."

"But you're only a street away."

*She looked up the address?*

"I'll get my coat and be right over."

"Hurry. I need someone to talk to. "

He hung up gently, wondering at the muted anticipation he thought he heard in her voice, not daring to think it was eagerness. *Don't flatter yourself, dummy, it's probably just nerves or something.*

*But why would she call?*

He'd known too many disappointments in the past not to minimize the significance of her invitation. And yet, he stood motionless for a time, pondering the riddle of her eyes.

Against such odds, the Void didn't stand a chance.

On his way over, he wondered whether he should invite her to the Sons meeting the following evening. *A joint invitation would be more proper, but maybe he'll be too busy campaigning. Or he might not like Laurel and Hardy.*

He thought of his father. *What would he call her, half-a-goy or half-a-Jew? Why should I care?*

It took four minutes to slop through the half-frozen streets to the Rushes' apartment building. En route, he examined the idea that had been niggling away at the back of his mind.

On closer scrutiny, he realized there was more than one posssibility. It was almost like computing a 2 per cent saline solution, or figuring one of those head-splitters they used to toss at him at Temple: "Dissolve $1\frac{1}{2}$ grams of boric acid in 40cc of water. How much more water must be added to make a 50cc solution?" Given the proper information, the process should always produce the correct answer.

*Only it doesn't.*

The doorman took his name and announced his arrival.

*Why the hell won't she look at me?*

For the fourth time, he noticed her glance nervously at the front door. *If she's afraid her husband'll walk in, why'd she bother to invite me in the first place?*

Not that they were doing anything wrong. He sat on a huge orange sofa-shaped bolster called a Lofa and tried to keep from spilling scotch on the fabric. Melinda, demure in pale-green pants suit, was perched across from him on the edge of a pumpkin-colored easy chair, on which she looked uneasy.

The initial flood of reminiscence had already ebbed. There was an awkward silence. She sipped Dubonnet-with-a-twist and stole surreptitious peeks at the door.

*Who's she expecting?*

"I forgot to thank you, Marty."

"What for?"

"For going after Lukas yesterday." She spoke softly and did not look at him.

He shrugged. "Nobody else was about to budge."

"True." She hesitated, then spoke again. "Why did you go?"

"Why?" he echoed. *Doesn't she know?* He swallowed scotch before replying. "I went because you asked."

"But you're not family. There wasn't any reason for you to become involved." Her eyes were still downcast. Her voice was as remote as if she were a holograph projected from a distant star.

*No reason for me to get involved?*

A long, embarrassing silence.

*What the hell should I do, change the subject? Yap about old-time movies? Dredge up another stale name from high school? Or just go?*

It was she who finally spoke. "My mother did mention you several times. I didn't make the connection, though, who you were."

"We saw each other practically every day. I liked her a lot."

"Then you belong to a small, exclusive club," she said with muted bitterness.

"Uh, yeah. I noticed your relatives keep their emotions pretty well under control."

She laughed mirthlessly. "What emotions?" She finished her wine. "Oh, I know Lukas was very upset to find her like that, but now he's too worried about his personal situation for any feelings to be left over. My oldest sister hasn't had anything to do with my mother for years, and Dinah deliberately exiled herself to make things easier."

"I'm afraid I don't follow," said Marty.

"There's no reason to. I shouldn't air family secrets in public." She rose, went to a sideboard in the next room and refilled her glass. "Do you want more scotch?"

He nodded. Maneuvering with difficulty off the Lofa, he joined her and, at her invitation, freshened his own drink. "*My* mother," he remarked, taking some ice, "used to know Mrs. Fenimore, and she mentioned part of your family history. Said you're all half Jewish."

"We're not."

"But I thought—"

"You thought what people usually think. Mama was

Jewish when she got married, so everyone who wants to give us that label does. It doesn't matter what a person really regards herself as."

"Well, then, what *are* you?"

"Nothing," Melinda stated.

"You mean you're an atheist?" he asked slowly.

"No. I'm nothing. *Nothing.*"

They returned to the living room.

"My mother felt guilty about giving up her religion for my father," Melinda explained. "After he died, she came down on us kids to switch. Lukas did, for a while. My sisters refused."

"And you?"

"To keep peace, I kept my mouth shut about what I thought. I pretended to do whatever she wanted. But after what happened to Dinah, I decided, that's it, no more religion, period. It's not worth the heartache."

"All right, but what happened to your sister? You can't tell me that much, then leave me hanging."

Melinda sighed. "All right. I guess I have a big mouth. First of all, Regina married Bill McKaye, which infuriated Mama. 'There's not enough Jewish doctors?' You can imagine. Regina, of course, is strong. The two of them had arguments, or maybe it was just one long argument, and in the end, they weren't speaking at all. But Dinah is a lot weaker. She married a Catholic. My mother took everything out on her, and finally her husband left her. Who could blame him? There was a divorce, and Dinah ran away half across the country."

Marty took a deep breath. *And the old lady seemed so sweet.* "How about you?"

"Me? My husband was born Jewish, never mind that

he doesn't go to synagogue. The label satisfied my mother."

"So you stayed in her good graces."

"Me and Lukas. He lived at her place for a long while."

"Until your mother kicked him out."

It surprised her. For a fleeting instant she looked in his eyes. He felt a bit giddy. *Too much scotch.* "How did you know about that?" she asked.

"Lukas mentioned it yesterday. He didn't tell me why it happened. I guess he decided not to stay Jewish, huh?"

"Well, that was part of it." She did not volunteer any further information.

Their eyes met again. Neither spoke.

*Why does she look at me like that?*

There was a line of verse his roommate sometimes quoted that occurred to him. It had something to do with a woman's glance meaning little or nothing or much.

"Strange," she murmured, looking down again.

"Strange?"

"How little we know about each other."

"You and I?"

She shook her head. "All of us."

A key turned in the front lock. Marty started, almost jumped up.

"They're here," she said, sounding a bit relieved.

"Who?" His voice was a bit higher than usual.

The door opened. In filed Dinah Fenimore and her sister Regina, followed by the stout Amish-farmer-look-alike, Dr. William McKaye. Steven Rush entered last and shut the door.

*What in all hell is this?*

"I see you succeeded," Regina told Melinda, indicating

Marty with a short, contemptuous glance in his direction.

Melinda nodded but did not reply. She got up and helped her eldest sister remove her coat, all the while assiduously avoiding Marty's questioning gaze.

He rose. Setting his glass on a side table, he faced the group and asked for the meaning of the unexpected conclave. Melinda still wouldn't look at him, but everyone else returned his stare with thinly veiled hostility.

"You'd better sit down," the doctor suggested. His voice was harsh, unfriendly.

"I'll stand. What's going on?"

Regina sat in the pumpkin chair, motioning her husband to stand by her side. "I told my sister to call and invite you here. After you accepted, Steven drove over and picked up the rest of us."

"I'm staying with them," the blonde volunteered with a nervous smile. *As false as her boobs.* She rested on the Lofa next to Melinda. Rush walked to the stairway and sat on the second step.

Marty looked from one to the other. "I still don't see why you all wanted me here." He addressed Regina. "Why didn't you call me yourself if you wanted to talk to me?"

"I don't even know you," she said airily.

"I suggest you be seated," her husband repeated. Standing stiffly by his wife, he might have been posing for an antique daguerrotype. "This may take some time."

"*What* may?" Marty demanded.

Regina said, "*We* think you are responsible for our mother's death."

Marty didn't trust himself to answer at first. When he

did, it was solely to Melinda. "So this is what you think?" he asked. "That I'm capable of murder?"

"I don't know," she murmured, almost imperceptibly shaking her head.

"Nobody called you a murderer," her husband said quickly. "All my sister-in-law meant is she thinks you *might* have been responsible."

*Distorting evidence, aren't you, counselor? But a slander suit would stink at the polls.*

"So," Marty addressed the rest of them, "you all decided to come over and hold a kangaroo court. You say I'm responsible, but you're not calling me a murderer. Would you care to explain?"

The matronly Regina nudged her husband, saying, "You should handle this."

The doctor nodded; tugging abstractedly at his beard, he spoke. "Mrs. Fenimore died of a drug reaction. You were her pharmacist. This is a busy time of year. Isn't it possible you might have made some mistake?"

"Not a mistake," Regina said coldly, "negligence."

The attorney hushed her, but she ignored him.

"Well, Mr. Gold?" Regina demanded. "Can you deny the possibility of such an error?"

"Yes," Marty heatedly retorted, "and I'll tell you exactly why." He launched into a detailed explanation of the police's hypothesis of how the drug entered the victim's system. He cited Etta Spector's eyewitness account of his innocence of negligence. He told them of the pill he'd given Mrs. Fenimore on Thanksgiving morning.

"If you rule out mistakes," he said finally, "and if she didn't commit suicide, then she was murdered. I don't know who did it, but *I* sure didn't have any good reason to, and I was occupied during the time it probably was done. Can you all say the same?"

He stopped then. Melinda was silently crying.

A long silence. Slowly, one by one, the family turned to Regina. She looked as grim as an inquisitor condemning a heretic.

She weighed the decision, then pronounced it. "There is nothing we can do."

"We have to!" Melinda exclaimed. "It wasn't him!"

"How do you know?" her husband asked. "Look at the way he behaved yesterday."

"He loved Mama!"

"Did he?" It was Regina. "Odd how he expressed it."

"*You* should talk!" Melinda snapped. "You hated her."

Regina did not deign to reply.

"Can someone tell me," Marty interrupted, "what you're all talking about?"

"My brother," Melinda said. "They arrested him."

*Oh? And you wanted me for his scapegoat?*

"I'm surprised," Marty said sarcastically, looking from the McKayes to Dinah, "that the three of you bothered to come over here for such a trivial reason."

The doctor stared at him stonily, but it was Regina who spoke. "Mr. Gold, I regard you as a total stranger. You will kindly refrain from intruding on family business."

Marty strode over to her, seething. Rush quickly stood up, but the pharmacist stopped about a foot away from Regina and regarded her with disdain. "You have a hell of a nerve getting your sister to drag me over here and then telling me to butt out! You accuse me of negligence in professional duty, imply (is that the word, counselor?) that I killed your mother, *and now you expect courtesy?*

You know what I think, lady? You wanted to accuse me, not because of your brother, but just to avoid the publicity. It might be embarrassing at your husband's clinic!"

Regina's face whitened. Her husband's flushed.

*Bull's-eye. Two checkerboard squares.*

"You know what it's like having to defend yourself to people you don't even know or like? I'll show you! Answer some of *my* questions. Where were all of you the night before your mother died?" He pointed at the nervous blonde. "What conditions do you have to fill to get your full income from the estate? Promise not to marry another *goy*? How about you, Doctor? Will anything stick to your fingers when you take care of your mother-in-law's holdings? Is that what you whispered to your wife yesterday when she was going to yelp about being left out of the will?"

Regina was on her feet. "Bring my coat, Melinda." She glowered at Marty. "You're very rude."

*And you're a nasty bitch! And built like a bathtub.*

But he stopped himself from answering in kind. It was, after all, Melinda's home and Regina was her sister. Besides, he was overcome all at once with a wave of tiredness and apathy. *I just want to go to bed.*

The McKayes and Dinah Fenimore quickly donned coats, hats and scarves. No one spoke. But the blonde, on an impulse, suddenly stepped up to the pharmacist and, smiling nervously, said, "I wasn't even here Friday. Yesterday I missed—"

"Dinah," Regina snapped, "we're going!"

The blonde seemed embarrassed at her sister's peremptory tone, but she obeyed it.

"I'll phone you tomorrow," Regina told Melinda, then, dismissing her, stepped through the door.

Steven Rush closed and locked it after they were gone. He gestured to Marty, who was getting his own coat.

"Don't go yet," Rush said. "I know we owe you an apology." He gestured toward the sideboard. "After that ordeal, a drink is the only merciful thing I can think of!"

Marty nodded. "I was working on your scotch."

Rush went into the next room and dropped ice in a fresh glass. Melinda sat on the Lofa, a worried expression on her face.

"Mind if I sit back down?" Marty asked, not waiting for the permission to be granted.

She looked at him anxiously. "*You* don't think Lukas could do such a terrible thing, do you?"

"Why should my opinion matter? A few minutes ago, you were willing to believe *I* killed your mother."

"Please. I'm sorry." She brushed his hand lightly with her fingertips. It was the first time they had ever touched, and though it was the most trifling of intimacies, it had its effect on Marty.

Rush brought his drink, gave his wife more wine and sampled his own generous shot of Jack Daniels. Melinda took the glass and promptly forgot about it; it rested in her hand of its own weight.

"Do you think they have a case against Lukas?" Marty asked the attorney.

"Don't know. I'm not a policeman." He smoothed back the stray lock of hair, the one that reminded Marty of James Bond. "The only thing I could get out of Abe Chubb is that Lukas is being held for questioning. I guess the fact he found her body doesn't do him any good."

"I'm afraid he had a reason," said Marty.

"Oh?"

"He mentioned it yesterday. He owes money to an unsavory source."

"But he could have gotten money from Mama!" Melinda exclaimed.

"He didn't, though," Marty replied.

Melinda persisted. "Did he say anything else? Did he tell you where he was on Friday?"

"I didn't ask. I didn't stay long. The two of us didn't get along too well."

Marty paused to imbibe more scotch. He was beginning to feel rather lightheaded. His voice sounded far-off. *Better lay off before I get smashed.* He rarely drank. His father—who never had anything in the house but the sugary ceremonial wine he called "Kool-Aid with a kick"—had indoctrinated Marty in the biased belief that drinking was primarily a Gentile pursuit. "Jews don't get drunk," Gold often proclaimed righteously. "You ask any doctor, he'll tell you the majority of your winos are *goyim!*" Since Marty moved into his own apartment, he kept a few bottles of liquor handy, but they had been chosen at random, with no critical experience whatsoever, and his roommate consumed them far more than he. Marty's preferred drink was beer. It—

*Hold on.* A thought occurred to him.

"I just realized," he told Melinda. "There *is* my roommate."

"I don't understand."

"The big fellow you met yesterday. He went after Lukas with me."

"Oh, yes. What about him?"

"He stayed with your brother after I left, talked to him a while. Maybe he learned something I don't know about."

Setting her still-untouched drink on the floor, she impulsively pressed Marty's hand. His pulse quickened. "Is your roommate in now, do you think?"

"Maybe. He keeps weird hours. Want me to go home and call you if he is?"

"Phone him from here. Please?" she urgently pleaded.

"Sure. I could do that."

Rush finished his drink and yawned. "Excuse me," he apologized, "I'm dead on my feet. Would you mind if I go to bed? If you find anything out, my wife can let me know in the morning."

Marty said goodnight to him, and the attorney went upstairs to his bedroom. Meanwhile, Melinda was on her feet, heading toward the adjacent dining room. She gestured at a small desk covered with papers and flyers. "There's the phone."

He walked over to a pink Princess telephone resting on a partially unrolled campaign poster. He picked up the instrument to dial and the slick paper furled with a slight snap. The noise was surprisingly loud to Marty, and he realized he was getting a headache. *Even the sound of the dialing bothers me.* His line was busy. The buzz made him wince.

"He's talking to someone," he told Melinda. "He won't stay on long, he hates telephones. I'll call again in a couple of minutes."

On his way to the living room, he almost stumbled headlong onto the Lofa.

She grabbed his arm and helped him regain his balance. "Marty, what's wrong? Don't you feel well?"

"Drank too much. Sorry."

"Hush, it's not your fault." She rested her fingers briefly, very briefly against his lips. "I did a terrible thing, making you face my family like that. Can you forgive me?"

*Can I forgive you?* He was keenly aware of the gentle pressure of her hand on his arm. *Novelty, woman apologizing to me. Nice for a change.* Her wide eyes entreated, but he searched them for other things. He sensed how easily the tremulous set of her lips could change to a sorrowful pout. For no sensible reason, he suddenly pictured Carol Blum's head on Melinda's shoulders. *Ecch. Beast on the Beauty.*

He forgave Melinda, then, with a groan, asked if they could possibly sit down.

"Yes." She drew him onto the orange bolster, and they sat beside one another. A wordless moment elapsed, then she said softly, shyly, "Marty, I *am* happy to see you . . ." and was silent again.

Did he dare imagine some meaningful hint in her inflection? *But what should I say to her? Something clever. No, not clever—sincere. Let her know how I feel about her.* But the words eluded him. He closed his eyes to think, which was a mistake, for he was suddenly overcome with vertigo. He felt like he was plummeting through dark and endless depths. When he opened his eyes, the room was busily tilting. He willed it to grow steadier, but it refused to co-operate.

*Dummy, dummy, get hold of yourself! Talk to her, already!*

But the moment, such as it was, had already passed him by, and Melinda once more started talking about her brother.

"He was my mother's darling, 'the baby,' even after they had the fight and she threw him out of the house. It was still 'See Lukas gets this' and 'Watch Lukas doesn't hurt himself.' She never wanted to worry him. 'Don't tell him about Dinah's problem, he'll worry,' 'Don't let him know I'm sick, he'll worry,' 'Don't tell—'"

Marty broke in. "What *is* Dinah's problem?"

"She had a breakdown after her marriage dissolved. It was Mom's interfering more than anything that did it, but as far as she was concerned, Dinah was an alcoholic and that was that." Melinda glanced at her watch. "Do you think you could try your roommate again?"

Marty nodded, rose with great caution, and stepped carefully into the dining room.

Bill Finney answered on the second ring.

"Herr Gold!" he exclaimed. "I was worried. You never go out this late! The salami is practically gone."

"Never mind. I'm over at Melinda Rush's. Lukas has been arrested. Now listen—when you talked to him, did he tell you anything about where he'd been Friday night?"

"Hardly. It wasn't a question I would have been likely to pose."

"I didn't think so. But could he have said anything else that'd help him?"

The actor was silent a moment while he attempted to recall the previous day's conversation. "I'm afraid, Herr Gold, the only thing that might have some bearing is negative."

Marty, still dizzy, leaned against the wall to steady himself. "Let me hear it, Bill."

"Well, Lukas boasted he was the only one in the family whom his mother still allowed to possess a key to her apartment."

"*That's* not going to help his case a hell of a lot."

"I'm sorry I can't do better," Bill Finney said regretfully. "I can't believe Lukas is responsible."

"Yeah," Marty sighed. "Well, I'll see you later."

"Just a minute, sirrah. You had a message."

"Who from?"

"A Mr. Gallagher."

"Who?"

"Gallagher," his roommate repeated. "The doorman of Mrs. Fenimore's building."

"Oh. Cholly. What's that shlub want?"

"He asked if you were home. I said no. Then he wanted to know if you'd seen the ten o'clock news."

"I was just a little busy then," Marty said sourly. "Look, Cholly's a smart-ass. Was he being serious?"

"He sounded a little agitated."

"Hm. Well, what am I supposed to do, call him?"

"Yes. He left a number."

Marty wrote it down, hung up and dialed the exchange. It rang several times before Gallagher answered.

"Half out the door," he panted, "figured it was you. Listen, I'm workin' late shift, I gotta get goin'. Meet me in the lobby."

"Why?"

"Guy I told you about," he said, still short of breath. "One I seen visiting Old Lady Fenimore."

"The one in the trench coat?"

"Uh-huh. Look, I'm late, I'll be at the building, okay?"

"Yeah."

Cholly hung up.

Melinda greeted Marty expectantly as he re-entered the living room. "Did your roommate remember anything that could help my brother?"

"No, but something else came up. It might be important."

"What?"

"I'm leaving now to find out."

"Will you let me know what it is?"

"I'll call first thing in the morning."

"If it's bad, I still want to know. Promise?"

"Uh-huh."

Marty put on his overshoes and topcoat. At the door, Melinda thanked him for wanting to help, in spite of the shabby way he'd been treated. She tilted up her chin to kiss his cheek.

Before he realized what he was doing, Marty turned his head and met her lips with his.

*Brilliant, Romeo! You've screwed up everything!* He stepped back, stammered an apology and rushed out the door.

Melinda, startled at the liberty he'd taken, watched him hurrying down the hall toward the elevators. She was confused and did not know what to think.

Yet she was sure she was not angry.

New snow lay lightly on the city, and the distant noise of traffic on Broadway was muted by the deep whiteness into which his feet sank. On Riverside Drive a wilderness of frost-crystals sparkled in the feeble glow of streetlamps obscured by whirling snowflakes.

In the serene night air, Marty felt calmer, less ashamed of his impetuous kiss; the coldness was bracing and his head began to clear.

He was in no hurry to reach his destination. He stood cloaked in tree shadow on the river side of the Drive. Across the way he saw the building where Mrs. Fenimore once lived. Cholly Gallagher waited in the lighted vestibule, a newspaper under his arm.

He wondered whether he ought to bother with the rendezvous. *It's not any of my business any longer.*

But after a long, indecisive moment, Marty crossed the street, tracking an unwilling trail in the unsullied snow.

Cholly opened the door and Marty stepped into a small square alcove, two sides of which were glass walls, the remaining two consisting of the front door and the locked portal to the main lobby. The doorman stuck out his pink, chubby hand and heartily shook Marty's.

*Since when have we become so damn friendly?*

"Mart, I got the late edition after I saw the news." He opened the newspaper to an item on page five. "They flashed his picture on Channel Nine and I recognized him."

There was no photo in the newspaper. The story was

only three paragraphs long, hastily dashed off to get into the final press run.

### DETECTIVE MURDERED IN OFFICE

Police found the bloody corpse of a Manhattan private detective this evening. The victim was shot to death in his own 83rd Street business office.

Jacob (Jack) Cohen, 42, of 910 West 83rd St. (at West End Ave.), was discovered dead of several gunshot wounds of the head and chest. None of the building staff or his neighbors heard any shots, according to the police, and the Medical Examiner estimates Cohen's body may have lain undetected for upwards of 72 hours.

The deceased sleuth may have been murdered by one of his clients. Efforts are being made to find out what cases Cohen was investigating at the time of his death; however, there is evidence his files have been tampered with, presumably by his assassin.

"And this is the guy you let in to see Mrs. Fenimore?" Marty asked.

Cholly nodded. "Sure looked like 'im on the news."

"Then he probably was killed by the same person."

"Uh-huh."

"So why'd you call me instead of getting in touch with the police?"

Cholly playfully punched Marty's shoulder, which only

## My Son, the Druggist

succeeded in annoying him. "Jeez, Mart, I figured it'd be better comin' from you. Y'know?"

"I don't see how."

"Look, what I mean is I feel bad about gettin' you in hock with the fuzz. I know you ain't somebody that goes around croakin' old ladies, so I wanted to make it up to you. If you give this to the cops, they'll figure you're clear. I mean, if you did it, you wouldn't go pointin' out the connection between this Cohen stiff and old lady Fenimore, would you?"

Marty stared at him coldly. "This is the first time, Cholly, you ever gave a damn what happens to me."

"Aaah, Christ, Mart, you still sore about crap that happened almost ten years ago? Jeez, I used t'fool around, so what?" He looked genuinely hurt. "You gonna hold it against me all my life?"

*God almighty! The shlub's got feelings.*

"Okay, Cholly, okay." Marty tried to soothe Gallagher's ruffled sensitivities. "Sorry I got ticked off, it's been a lousy night all around." He yawned. "I've gotta get some rest. Look, I appreciate your trying to help. I'll call the cop first thing tomorrow."

"Lemme know what happens."

"Sure."

Cholly thrust his hand forward. "No hard feelings, Mart?" he asked, his flabby lips twisted in an uncertain grin.

"Yeah, Cholly, no hard feelings." He shook his hand, half-expecting it to contain a joy buzzer.

*Okay. So I don't hate the dope. Friends with him, though, I'm still not.*

Cholly opened the door for him, and Marty started

down the front steps, but before he reached the sidewalk, the doorman hailed him and he stopped.

"What?"

"Better take the paper, Mart," he suggested. His voice seemed loud in the hush of the winter night. "You're liable to forget the name."

"I remember it. Jack Cohen."

"Take it anyhow, just in case." Gallagher walked down the steps, stuck the newspaper out for Marty to grasp. He reached for it, but before he was able to grab hold, it fell to the ground.

So did Cholly.

Marty spun around, his ears ringing with the explosion. Bewildered and frightened, he peered into the darkness, but saw no one.

Cholly moaned. Marty stooped to see if he could help, and as he did, a second bullet slammed into his back, hurling him forward into the snow that was no longer colorless.

Hurrying footsteps. He could not see the person who gathered up the fallen newspaper. A whistle shrilled, and then another . . . another . . . the sound of running, quickly fading . . . an eerie ululation, a siren . . .

And then he heard no more.

*Hayeled. Hayaldoh.*

Every time he finished filling the bottle, she looked at him appealingly and he sloshed the liquid over the edge, ruining the label, which he'd laboriously prepared in Hebrew script, but her glance broke his rhythm and he lost the bid for the Basie after the bitch fell asleep in the middle of the service.

*Mendele Godolkin.*

"Martin, listen to me, your father hates to wear ties!"

*Mendele Godolkin.*

But he could not come to the altar because he wasn't finished at work, and Spector wouldn't give him an extension of Snowden's Paradise Orchestra, so the liquid sloshed and ruined the Hebrew label, and he was afraid to say what he believed because it was wishful thinking and his father interrupted, very loud.

"Marty, you can hear? I'm talking." *He sounds worried.*

"Abe, shah!" his mother whispered.

*Yeah, Pop, shah!*

Silence.

Her face, suspended in space, looming closer, her eyes questioning. Fading.

*Come back, I'm sorry!*

"For what, Martillah?" It was Herbie. "Yiddishe guilt? You get a kick in the rear and you apologize for sticking it in the way of the foot."

Darkness.

He couldn't get an extension of time on the Basie bid,

and his father called him to the altar, but he couldn't take off his shoes, they were wet with snow, but her glance broke his rhythm and the blonde wouldn't let him come up and the liquid spilled and ruined the label.

His brother's face. Another phantom?

"Yussie?" His own voice was so feeble it might have surprised him, but he was too enervated to care.

His brother nodded.

"Back so soon?"

*Who's crying?*

"I came when I heard what happened, Marty. They gave me special leave."

Silence again. Once more, darkness. The confusion of images had another chance to play countless variations.

Meanwhile, the staff at Jacobson Polyclinic gave him two transfusions, treated him for shock, set a chipped bone, frequently administered sedatives and constantly monitored his pulse and blood pressure.

His eyelids flickered. His mother, leaning over him, brushed his hair back gently with her hand . . . *goddamn cowlick* . . . and he was asleep again.

The next afternoon, Marty was finally able to relate to his surroundings. He opened his eyes and waited for the pale-green wall and cream-colored ceiling to come into focus.

"Marty?" It was his brother. "You hear me?"

"Yuss," he croaked, "you *are* here."

"Who'd you expect?" his brother grinned in relief.

"Ma?"

"She's down in the coffee shop. She'll be back in a while. How you feel?"

"Funny. Doped."

## My Son, the Druggist

"Why not? They've got enough sedation in you to support a junkie for a year."

The effort of talking exhausted him. His head lolled sideways on the pillow. The angle helped him see his brother's face more clearly.

"You're tan," he murmured.

"Georgia sun," his brother laughed. He was nineteen, slim and slight, with clear blue eyes, light hair cut shorter than usual by the army, and an overbite that always was visible since he rarely stopped smiling. Though he was extremely worried about his brother, he was too buoyant to let his concern show.

"You've got a ton of cards," he said, gesturing to the windowsill. "Want to hear some?"

Marty shrugged, a slight movement.

"Okay. Here's one from Viv." He plucked one off the sill and opened it. "Want the poem or just the message?"

"Message."

"'Dear Kid-Brother-Number-One, didn't Mom tell you not to play in the street?' All heart, as usual." He picked up a second card, scanned it. "Aunt Bea wants you to come visit when you get well."

"Why?"

"What else? Her niece Lilah . . ."

There were similar messages from his cousin concerning a friend named Myrtle and from his grandmother, whose husband's lodge brother Sid Chalfin had a daughter, Audrey, who wanted to meet the hero . . .

*Always matchmakers, always dogs.*

There was a personal note from Lou and Etta Spector, a handwritten scrawl from his roommate and a tall contemporary card with a suggestive poem and picture inside, Herbie's, of course. A flowery one from Betty, Herbie's friend.

Marty drifted off again before his brother was finished.

When he awoke, he felt stronger. His brother was talking to someone, but they were over on the other side of the room, and Marty couldn't see. Then he recognized his roommate's voice.

"Perhaps, Lieber Gold-Bruder, I should return at a more opportune time."

He called Bill Finney, and both he and Marty's brother turned. The actor's face looked delighted.

"Herr Gold! You have rejoined us?"

Marty struggled to sit up. His brother put a restraining hand on his shoulder.

"Relax. There's no place for you to go."

"Bill," said Marty, "I have to talk to you. Help me sit up."

"Not now, not now," his brother tried to calm him, but Marty insisted on sitting up, so Bill Finney slid an arm beneath his back and carefully got him into a more upright position.

"I *could* just crank up the bed," his brother suggested.

"Forget it, Yussie. I want to be able to see Bill's face, not his belly."

"An upsetting view, surely," Finney said wryly.

"Bill, listen," Marty began, but the effort of talking and sitting up had sapped his scant strength. Swallowing with difficulty, he asked his brother for water.

"You might like to know, Friend Apothecary," Finney said while Marty sipped, "your bid won the Basie. I opened it to make sure it survived the postal cretins. I believe you'd say it's in mint condition."

The news would have delighted him at another time, but now Marty merely nodded and asked, "How's Cholly?"

Bill Finney glanced over at Marty's brother, but neither spoke.

*Oh, Christ!*

"Come on, come on, did he make it?"

His roommate shook his head.

Even though he knew what the answer would be, it was still a shock.

*And just because he wanted to help me.*

"Marty? You okay?"

*The poor shlub. At least we shook hands . . .*

"Marty?"

"Yeah, Yussie, I'm all right. I used to hate the slob."

A long silence.

"But for the grace of God," his brother murmured.

Marty stared at him, not trusting himself to reply.

*Which god, Yussie? The goy-killer or the Jew-saver?*

The door opened. When his mother saw him, she flew to the bedside and hugged him.

"Easy, Ida," Abe Gold cautioned, a big smile on his face, "you'll break another one of the bum's ribs."

For several minutes, they talked of small, unimportant things, topics his mother chose to keep Marty cheerful. All the while they chatted, his father held his son's hand tightly in his.

At last, a nurse suggested they clear out and let Marty rest. His father and brother told him to take it easy and promised to come back that evening. Bill Finney started to leave with them, but Marty asked him to wait a moment.

His mother lingered until her husband was no longer in the room. Then she leaned over and spoke in a low voice. "Martin, you shouldn't worry, your father's not mad at you no more."

*No! Not really? Maybe I didn't notice, Ma?*

"So now that's off your mind, you just lay here and think over what we were talking about and what I told you because when you get out, *later*, then your father's going to start up again, don't think he won't. But now you're flat on your back, there's nothing stopping you from thinking all about a life of ritual." She held up a finger to emphasize her words. "And remember, Marty, remember, every smart person questions things sometime or other. Keep that in mind. It's not wrong to question. Sooner or later, smart people work things out and realize that thousands of years of tradition can't be wrong."

Marty said nothing. Bending, she kissed him on the forehead, said goodbye and left the room.

"Bill," he asked his roommate, "is it only Jews who think they know all the answers?"

Finney shook his head. "'All, all of a piece throughout,' he paraphrased, "their chase has a beast in view. The devout are all smug, *mein freund*, but you must understand that smugness is not an adjunct to a life of ritual, it is an integral part."

Marty nodded. "I guess so. Everybody thinks they're the chosen people."

"Amen." Bill Finney jerked a thumb at the door. "The nurse'll probably be in any second to chase me out. Was there something in particular you wanted me to do?"

"Uh-uh," Marty murmured, eyes closed. He was very tired. "Call the cop for me. I have to talk to him."

Although it was December, Inspector Abner Chubb was sweating. He regarded Marty with a mixture of annoyance and concern.

"Look, I can't just go making an arrest without some kind of proof. Sure, I thought of him, but I can't find any record of a gun, and the motive's all conjecture. He doesn't have any decent alibis, I'll admit, but neither does Lukas. And *he*, at least, had a motive."

"Yeah," said Marty, "but Lukas was locked up when me and Cholly were shot."

They were alone in Marty's room at Jacobson Polyclinic. Chubb had left word with the staff that he wanted to talk to the invalid when he'd recovered enough to see him. But it was Bill Finney who got in touch with the policeman, and the doctor refused to admit Chubb until the day after Marty asked his roommate to call.

There was a tap on the door and a nurse stuck in her head.

"You have another visitor, Mr. Gold."

"Who?"

"A Mrs. Rush."

*Melinda.* He looked at Chubb, but the policeman just shrugged.

"I guess you can show her in," Marty said.

Melinda entered at once. Her face was chalky, partly because she had no make-up on, and there were unaccustomed frown lines creasing the flesh above her lips.

"I'm sorry I couldn't visit you any sooner," she said as

she approached Marty's bedside. "I was awfully worried about you." Then she noticed the inspector seated in the corner chair. "Pardon me, are you still busy? I can come back in a while."

"Maybe it's a good thing you're here, Mrs. Rush," Chubb told her with great deliberateness, "Mr. Gold was just saying some interesting things about your husband."

*The ever-tactful fuzz!*

"What about my husband?" she asked, the frown lines deepening.

"I think," said Chubb, gesturing toward Marty, "it would come better from him."

*Thanks, loads!*

"Inspector," Marty asked, "could I talk to her alone, please?"

The policeman might have argued, but he found it hard to use his official intimidating manner with cleared suspects, so he let it go.

"I'll be right outside," he said, closing the door behind him.

An awkward pause.

"Well?" Melinda prompted him.

*She's not going to help me out at all.*

"Don't you know?"

She shook her head. "Don't play games, Marty. Say it."

*Ask me to punch you, why not, while I'm at it.*

He couldn't bring himself to state it directly, bluntly.

"It all fits together, don't you see?" Marty asked. "Somebody must've taken a couple of your mother's Darvon, emptied them and refilled them with Butazolidin dumped out of those capsules. They were both in easy access in her medicine chest. But if that's the way it happened—and it's the only plausible way—then it rules out nearly everybody."

"Why?"

"Because your sister Dinah wasn't even in New York until she heard about your mother's death. Regina and Dr. McKaye haven't spoken to your mother for years, and you said Lukas didn't know about her earlier allergic reaction."

"I might have mentioned it to Regina."

"You might've," Marty nodded, "but I was pretty sure the killer was a man."

"I don't see how you could know that."

"Mainly because of something your mother said the last time I saw her." He waited for Melinda to comment, but she didn't, so he continued, albeit unwillingly. "Mrs. Fenimore was more than usually glum Thanksgiving morning, I remember thinking, and when I asked her, she said it was family problems. Since the others are incommunicado, what she said must've applied either to you and your husband, or Lukas."

"*We* always got along with Mama," she objected, worriedly biting at her lower lip.

"Well, whoever was giving her the *tsooris*, she wouldn't talk about it to me, and that was very strange because she always told me her troubles. So I guessed it had to be pretty serious." *Damn cop. He had to stick me with this job. I'd rather chew on a vintage Gennett.* Marty's throat was sore from talking; he poured himself a drink of water, drank some, then resumed. "Your mother always used to kid me about becoming a part of your family. I thought she meant as a son. It didn't occur to me she might be displeased with her sons-in-law."

"She wasn't," said Melinda, "not with Steve."

He ignored the remark. "That morning, she said something odd. Before she left the store, she grabbed my hand and made me promise her I would never be a bum. Those were her words: "Promise me you'll never be a bum." She never did or said anything like that to me before, and she was definitely in earnest."

"So?" Melinda challenged. "What's it supposed to mean?"

"Your mother was Jewish, you never heard the expression? From my own family, I've noticed, in the Jewish vernacular, the word 'bum' usually means one thing. A man who fools around, a philanderer."

She said nothing.

"A woman is a tramp, a man's a bum, so that points to Lukas or the doctor or your husband. Lukas, I figure your mother knew all about him."

"What do you mean?" Melinda asked, her breath catching in her throat.

"I'm guessing the real reason she threw him out of her house."

*Yeah, I thought so. Her eyes tell me I'm right.*

"She wasn't speaking to the doctor, but even if she heard something about him, I'd imagine it would have pleased her. Something to use to try to break up that marriage. But she was upset about the situation. Who else is there but her one good son-in-law, the man she trusted?"

Melinda shook her head. "How could she have found out? She couldn't."

*Found out? Does that mean you know he's a cheat?* He remembered the fleeting moment in the chapel, the stifled argument between the Rushes. *Paying too much atten-*

tion, maybe, to Dinah? That why she didn't catch the first plane back, like she originally planned?*

"I don't know how she could have found out," Marty said, "but New York isn't so big when you're running for office in it. She might've been told by one of her old friends from the temple. The Jewish information service is pretty formidable, believe me, *I* know."

Melinda sat down, removed a pack of filters from her purse and tried to light one. She was so nervous it took three matches to manage the job. "Marty," she said, "I'm trying to listen to you with an open mind, but my God, you're telling me my husband killed my mother."

*How can she not believe it?*

"Why would he do it? To keep her from hurting him at the polls?"

"The polls," Marty agreed, "and his marriage, maybe."

"But how could she prove it to anyone?"

"By hiring a private detective."

She stared at him in disbelief. "If she did, where is this detective, then? Why doesn't he come forward and testify?"

"Because," he murmured, looking down, "he's dead."

There was such a lengthy silence that he finally looked up. Melinda was staring at him; he'd never seen such an expression on her face before.

*Does she hate me now? Or is it fear?*

He wished he was anywhere else, at the beach, at his sister's place in Washington, even at the store getting an earful from the Old Lady. But there was no backing out, so he told Melinda about the clipping Cholly Gallagher had shown him.

"Your mother must have hired this Jack Cohen, and

when he got something on your husband, she phoned and threatened him. Maybe she said she'd ruin his chances of election unless he granted you a divorce. I don't know. Whatever it was, she must have scared the hell out of him, because he apparently showed up Thanksgiving night prepared to poison her."

"You're just guessing! You can't know these things!"

"Melinda, look, the doorman was away from his post only once that night. Some kid ran into the lobby and made him mad enough to chase him down the street. What if your husband was afraid of being seen going up to your mother's? Couldn't he have given the kid money to pull the trick and get Cholly out of the lobby for a few seconds?" *If she'd cry or something, instead of just staring at me like a zombie.* "He probably didn't meet Cohen till he got up to the apartment, so he must've had to do some fast work finding out who he was, where he had his office. I don't know when he shot him, but it must've been soon, maybe even that night. Where the gun came from, I don't know, either, but he has one, I'm sure, because he came after me and Cholly so we wouldn't tell the police of the connection between the two murders."

"Marty," Melinda said in a tone of voice that made him stop to pay close attention. She hesitated. "I don't know how to put this . . ."

"Just say it."

"That night, when you kissed me, it was the first time I realized you—" She completed the thought with a gesture, rather than words. "Anyway, I was confused. I admit I liked it. But liking is one thing, breaking up a marriage is another . . ."

*That's what you think I'm doing? And that's why you're so agitated?*

"Marty, isn't it possible you're letting yourself be swayed in your thinking? What you've told me so far is all supposition."

"There's one thing I haven't mentioned yet," he said quietly. "I was just about to bring it up to the inspector when you came in."

"What?" she asked in a small voice. She stubbed out her cigarette.

"The night I went to meet Cholly, I spoke to him on your phone and made the appointment to see him over at the Riverside Drive building. You were in the other room, and I wasn't talking loud, so nobody could have possibly known I was going to meet him—"

"Which shows it must've been some maniac who shot at you!"

"No, it proves you must have an upstairs telephone extension."

She argued desperately, "It still could've been some lunatic, the city is full of them!"

Marty slowly shook his head. "A nut would've fired and run off—not stop to grab the paper."

A sharp intake of breath. "*What* paper?"

"The newspaper with the story in it about the murder of Jack Cohen. Cholly was just handing it to me when the bullet hit him, and he dropped it in the snow. Then, after—"

He stopped. She was trembling violently.

"Oh, god," Melinda murmured, her voice a monotone, devoid of life, "oh, god." Her shoulders shook. She closed her eyes, leaned her head on one hand. Marty wished he could get out of bed and put an arm round her.

"Well?" he asked, gently prodding. "*You* have to say, if you know something . . ."

"Yes. Yes! *Yes*," she repeated, "but don't you know what you're asking, Marty? Yes, he's been unfaithful, yes, he's lied to me, but he's my husband just the same. I've eaten a thousand meals with him, made love with him, fell asleep crying with his arms protecting me against the darkness." She paused. There were no tears. Her pale face resembled a death mask. "Yes," the dead voice resumed, "he owns a gun, a war trophy. Untraceable, he told me once. Yes, there's a phone extension in his den—and a door to the outside hall. When I went upstairs that night, he was just entering. His coat was on." Opening her eyes, she appealed to Marty. "You have to believe me, I didn't know. I *didn't*."

*You mean you didn't want to know.*

"You might have guessed something."

"I tried not to."

"But now you've changed your mind?"

She nodded.

"Why?"

Her reply was almost inaudible. "When I saw him coming in from outside, I asked him where he'd gone to so late, and he claimed he went out to buy a newspaper. He had one under his arm."

Melinda shuddered.

"It . . . it was very wet."

On the night of December twenty-fourth, Marty Gold stayed till closing, in spite of arguments from everyone. He'd been back at work for three days, but up till then Spector had sent him home each time after a few hours. That evening, however, Marty was adamant.

"Go home," the Old Lady told him at five o'clock. "I don't want you should plotz in my lap."

"It's the busiest day of the year. I'm staying."

At six, Herbie said, "Go home. You're dead on your feet."

"Tomorrow I'll sleep late."

It was Spector's turn at seven. "You're run down, you'll catch pneumonia. You'll survive, of course, but meanwhile you'll give it to me and I'm an *alte cocker* who won't stand a chance."

Marty laughed. "Lou, fifty years from now you'll still be here, stuffing pills."

"Wish such a fate on me again," growled Spector, waving his fist beneath Marty's nose, "and guess *where* I'll stuff pills. Now get the hell outta here."

But Marty refused to budge.

It soon became very busy at Spector's Drugs and nobody had time to nag Marty again, so he stayed till Spector shut and locked the door at nine. Just before he did, Marty sold the fifty-dollar bottle of perfume to a drunk. When Lou heard about it, he stuck out his tongue at Herbie and gave him a chorus of I-told-you-so's.

It was another twenty minutes before all of the customers in the store could be served, but at last Marty filled his final prescription of the day, hung up his jacket and prepared to leave.

Spector nudged Herb Adelstein, and the young man called, "Yo, Martillah, wait up, I'll walk you home."

"What am I, your date?" Marty protested. "I won't drop dead on the way."

"With your penchant for catching loose lead," Herb remarked, "I wouldn't tempt the furies. Let's go."

They bid the Spectors goodnight and left. Outside, Marty's brother stood waiting.

"Yussie! Why didn't you come on in?"

"Too stuffy. Hey, how about a beer, Marty?"

"Sure, Yuss, only I'm beat, let's have it at my place."

"Told you to go home early," Herb grumbled.

When they entered the apartment, the first thing that greeted their collective eyes was the awesome spectacle of Bill Finney standing by the refrigerator finishing a Coke in one long, continuous swallow.

*How the hell's he do that?* Marty wondered for the fortieth time.

His roommate waved at them. "Gentlemen, well met. May I offer you something?"

"Everybody's in the mood for beer, Bill," said Marty. "I notice you're dressed, for a change."

"I'm not a polar bear. It's colder in here than a pilgrim's chaperone."

They all sat down. The actor brought glasses and bottles of Beck, and the next few seconds were taken up in cap-prying and bead-adjusting.

"Still feeling bad about the broad?" Herbie asked with his customary bluntness.

Marty shrugged. "No reason to be, I guess. Still . . ."

"The Jewish sense of guilt, Martillah. You do the right thing, then you pull yourself apart wondering what your responsibility really was. Masochism with a twist of Talmudic logic." Herbie took a long drink of beer, holding one finger in the air to retain his hold on the conversation. "On the other hand, maybe you just feel lousy because you think you screwed up your chances with her permanently."

"I don't want to talk about it."

"Who's he mean?" his brother asked Bill Finney.

"The woman in the case, Herr Gold-Bruder. One Melinda Fenimore Rush."

"Oh, her." He addressed Marty. "Pop'd love that, wouldn't he? I heard you had quite a scene couple of weeks ago."

"That was different, Yussie. Melinda's half Jewish. By birth, anyhow, but that's how Pop'd think of her." *Would he?*

"Prejudice, prejudice," Bill Finney murmured.

"What?" Marty asked. "Who do you mean? Not me."

"You. Me. All of us, Guidman Martin. Remember how you first described her to me? You saw her as a pair of breasts, a smile, an attractively curved derrière. That's prejudice. Originally, she saw *you* as a Senior . . . another prejudice. When your mother recounted the Fenimore family history, Melinda suddenly seemed attainable because she was 'a half Jew'—right?"

"Ease off," Marty objected. "How are you defining prejudice, anyway?"

"Reacting to what you think a person is, instead of discovering his or her true nature."

There was a deal of argument on the point. Marty turned to his brother and asked his opinion.

"Me?" he smiled, a bit embarrassed. "I guess I agree with Bill. Down at Camp Benner, it's the first time I've been really treated like an alien. Starts you thinking." He shrugged. "I guess what it teaches you is if you think of yourself first as part of a group—*any* group—right away you're in a minority of your own making. If you're just a person, though, you're no longer part of a minority." He finished the rest of the liquid in his bottle. When he addressed his brother again, it was with considerable trepidation. "Marty, I . . . I hope you don't take this wrong, but I'd like to ask you a favor."

"Sure, Yussie, name it."

"That's it. Could you stop calling me Yussie? My real name is Joe, remember?"

*Oy!* "Correction. That's your American name."

His brother nodded. "But America is where I live." He stuck up a hand, forestalling Marty's inevitable comment. "No, I'm not ashamed of 'Yossele' and I'm not trying to bury my heritage. I'd just rather be called Joe."

*Uh-huh. Tell that to Pop.*

The phone rang.

"Must be Mom," said Marty, "inviting me for the tenth time to Sunday dinner."

"What do you expect?" Herb mocked. "You're now a hero. Till the Second Coming you'll be eating dinner with terriers."

Marty picked up the phone and said hello.

"Marty?" He knew who it was at once.

"Yes?" He tried to sound cool, aloof, for the benefit of the three men in the room with him.

"I've been away." Her voice was soft, as always. "I thought you might have tried to get in touch."

"No, that didn't happen," he replied nonchalantly. He avoided looking at his brother or friends. *If they ask, I'll say it's Dick about the Snowden disc.*

"I didn't think you would call, actually," Melinda said.

"Should I have?"

"I suppose it would have been . . . indiscreet."

"That's what I thought."

She was silent so long he thought she was no longer there, but then, abruptly, she spoke his name.

"Yes? What?"

"Should we care? What others think?"

*Me you ask? Me, the original Pharmacopoeia of Hang-ups?*

"Damned if I know," he said. "Wish I could tell what's important any more." Marty paused for the merest fraction of a second. "Of course, if you want, we *could* get together and talk about it." *Hooh-hah! You can't tell what's important, bubbaleh?*

"Yes," she said without hesitation, "I'd like that."

"When?"

"Tonight?"

"It's late." *What the hell do you call this? Déjà vu?*

"It's not too late for me," Melinda told him. "Where could we meet?"

"Not at your place."

"No. Not at yours, either."

*Already it starts?*

They agreed on the Café China near Eighty-seventh in

half-an-hour. Marty hung up and turned to look at Herbie, his brother Joe and his roommate, all of whom were curiously quiet.

"Something came up," Marty bluffed. "Record business." *Why bother? Look at their faces, they know.*

"Well," Herbie yawned, "I'm going home." He drank the rest of his beer and stood up. "Walking my way?" he asked Joe Gold.

"Yeah." He waved jauntily at his brother. "Listen . . . lots of luck, Marty."

Marty smiled rather sheepishly. "Thanks, Yuss (pardon me, Joe)—but for what?"

"How should I know?" His brother laughed. "With whatever you're going to need luck for."

With that, he said goodnight and left, Herb Adelstein in his wake.

As soon as they were gone, Marty turned to Bill Finney. "Well?"

"Well, sirrah?"

"Am I all that transparent?"

The actor made a courtly bow to his friend. "In all deference to your many superior qualities, Friend Martin, I should scarcely include opacity amongst your salient characteristics."

*He knows if he just plain answered "yes" I'd have a stroke.*

Bill Finney sat down. "Well, Herr Gold, shall we discuss't?"

Marty shook his head. "Not now, Bill, I want to get ready. Maybe when I get back."

"Excellent. I shall prepare an appropriate libation for the occasion."

*Thrill!*

But when he returned, his roommate was sound asleep and snoring. Marty was sorry he wasn't awake, since he felt like talking about the long conversation he'd had with Melinda.

*A lot of things to consider.*

But he was too tired, so he undressed, turned off the light and got into bed. There he lay, staring in the direction of the ceiling, which he could no longer see. Despite his great weariness, he could not fall asleep immediately. He thought of his mother, of that submissive relinquishment of authority that was her subtlest weapon of domination. His mind shifted to other memories, leaped from image to image, toyed with new ideas, pondered mysteries both ephemeral and eternal . . . and yet, inextricably tangled in the skeins of meditation, there was Melinda's face, flickering before him again and again in the darkness.

Slumber overtook him at last, but he was no nearer to solving the secret in the druggist's heart.

*Thursday, January 6*

*So, my dear Vivian,*

*All the messing around with the holidays is finally over, Yossele is off again for the rest of his term, and once more your father is yelling at your brother, the druggist. So what else is new?*

*You think I'm thrilled, maybe, the way Marty's acting? Let him be well and healthy, I love him, he's my flesh and blood, but believe me, such aggravation I never asked for. Your father is always hocking me, "Marty, this, Marty, that." Your brother could give me some peace already if he'd just settle his mind the way I told him. There's no excuse it should take so long.*

*I'm sorry I should burden you, because I can imagine you've got your arms full this week with returns and broken merchandise and getting ready for inventory, so I won't take any more of your time, honey, except to ask a favor of you.*

*I don't know if he's written and told you yet, but Marty is planning this spring to visit Washington for some meshuginah record convention. Records-shmecords, I used to throw those dust collectors out until your brother started treating them like a squirrel does his nuts.*

*Anyhow, when he comes, the favor I'm asking, is*

*maybe you could introduce your brother to some nice Yiddishe maidele? Even a few, perhaps? He's old enough, he should settle down soon, not run around with girls like I hear he's seeing. But that's none of my business, I wouldn't say a word, because one thing I'm glad I'll never be is an interfering mother.*

*All my love to you and Harold. Write soon.*

MAMA